WHEN WE ALMOST CAME UNDONE

WHEN WE ALMOST CAME UNDONE

GEORGIA K. BOONE

FEIWEL AND FRIENDS
NEW YORK

Content warning: This book contains references to a suicide attempt (not shown); depression; Covid-19/pandemic/lockdown era; police brutality (the murders of George Floyd and Breonna Taylor); the murders of Emmett Till and Trayvon Martin; racist and homophobic remarks; mental health issues; anxiety; overdosing on pills; and a family member in a coma.

A Feiwel and Friends Book
An imprint of Macmillan Publishing Group, LLC
120 Broadway, New York, NY 10271 · fiercereads.com

EU representative: Macmillan Publishers Ireland Ltd, 1st Floor, The Liffey Trust Centre, 117–126 Sheriff Street Upper, Dublin 1, D01 YC43

Library of Congress Cataloging-in-Publication Data

Names: Boone, Georgia K. author
Title: When we almost came undone / Georgia K. Boone.
Description: First edition. | New York : Feiwel and Friends, 2026. | Audience: Ages 13 and up | Audience: Grades 10–12 | Summary: As protests against police brutality, the COVID-19 pandemic, and her sister's depression upend her world, seventeen-year-old Tia struggles to hold on, but continues to find hope in her best friend and a new romance.
Identifiers: LCCN 2025039014 | ISBN 9781250834874 hardcover
Subjects: CYAC: COVID-19 Pandemic, 2020–2023 | Pandemics | Sisters | Friendship | LCGFT: Novels | Fiction
Classification: LCC PZ7.1.T876 Wh 2026
LC record available at https://lccn.loc.gov/2025039014

First edition, 2026
Book design by Maria W. Jenson
Feiwel and Friends logo designed by Filomena Tuosto
Printed in the United States of America

ISBN 978-1-250-83487-4
10 9 8 7 6 5 4 3 2 1

To my beloved sisters, without whom the stars
would cease to shine, and to my parents
and grandparents, who, despite all
the obstacles, continue ever forward

I hate when I'm supposed to be having fun and Race singles me out for special chores and duties.

—Margo Jefferson, *Negroland: A Memoir*

What is it you want me to reconcile myself to? . . . You always told me it takes time. It has taken my father's time, my mother's time, my uncle's time, my brothers' and my sisters' time, my nieces' and my nephews' time. How much time do you want for your "progress"?

—James Baldwin, *The Price of the Ticket*

CHAPTER ONE

MY SISTER ALEXIS SAYS FLUNKING OUT OF high school isn't an option. So, I'm sitting here forcing my eyes to stay open and pretending that Rebecca Tomlinson's top button isn't about to fly off while Greg and Eric make stupid faces at each other on this Zoom call. I finished our history final twenty minutes ago, but I still have to be on-screen to prove I didn't cheat.

I'm pretty sure sitting here in silence watching other people sit in silence is contributing to the death of my brain cells. But Alexis also says that half of professional success is learning how to bullshit; I guess this is an excellent primer. As soon as it hits eleven A.M., though, I click out of the screen and try not sink into a puddle of misery.

This is the *worst.*

Listen, it's not like I had big plans for senior year. I had absolutely zero intention of going to prom, I wasn't in any club or student council, and I barely managed to make it onto the B-team for volleyball. Still, there's something about leaving your house once in a blue moon that really brings a tear to your eye when you realize your graduation may be virtual, your first year of college might be virtual, and your kitchen counter is going to be your new best friend for at least the next year.

Thankfully, just as I'm about to bash my head against said counter, my actual best friend texts me. I know it's him because my phone makes a donkey sound every time his messages come through.

I guess a size D, easily.

You're awful.

Sorry. Had to be said. I could focus on literally nothing else.

Maybe we should start a clothing drive for Rebecca. She's clearly in need.

Probably. But maybe she doesn't need it. I heard the graduation ceremony might be in person.

Great! Wait. She's not going?

Health issues.

Damn. Now I feel bad for not reproaching your misogyny.

Consider me reproached.

Thanks.

This is nice. Texting like this, like normal. It's distracting me from the fact that I'm home right now instead of at the hospital, where I should be. Where we should all be, pacing and biting our nails, and waiting for my other sister, Mel, to wake up. We can't, though, because we're in the middle of an unpredictable hellscape with a mysterious sickness that no one's heard of before. Apparently, any of us could die from it—or we could pass it on to someone else, if we don't know we already have it. The infection lurks like a bandit in the night, ready to take over our lungs and suffocate us as we sleep. Or not. Depends on who you ask. Some people think the pandemic is a hoax, and we should all just go about our days as usual.

Either way, hospital visitation is severely limited, so I'm stuck at home, worrying about my sister while my best friend tries to distract me with zombie memes, because ha ha ha, we're all going to die anyway. It's much better than the other texts he's sent, trying to get me to go to one of the protests that have been blocking the streets for the past few days. It's not that I'm against them. It's more like I'm . . . over them.

Does it suck that an unarmed man was killed by police officers? One hundred percent. Does it suck that, like me, this dude was Black, which exactly no one should be shocked by? Also, one hundred percent. But he's not the first, and not the last, and I don't really have the energy. I don't know how anyone does. There have already been a jillion protests about wearing masks and quarantining and how asking people to do either is against our civil rights or whatever. And now this. All the protesting feels like an endless loop of dystopian torment from which I'd very much like to escape. Unfortunately, Drew doesn't exactly see my point of view.

We got into a big fight about it the day after George Floyd died, which was right after the complete and total radio silence we had right after the . . . well, the *other* thing. We were in English class together on Zoom, when one of our teachers decided that we should debate whether Black lives matter. Okay, fine, I mean, the teacher framed it as a debate around rhetoric and values—the protests about George's death versus the protests about wearing masks in the middle of a global pandemic—but then one kid likened the George protests to domestic terrorism, and another kid changed their screen name to "black rifles matter," and then our teacher said class was dismissed.

The next day, when Drew and I should've been rewatching *Hamilton* for the nineteenth time, he instead wanted to talk about some "action" that he and a bunch of other students from our class were planning, to "protest" what happened. And . . . fine. But I can't do it. Not right now. He said I was apathetic and then got mad when I said that he was trying to be a budget Malcolm X, and then we didn't talk again until I called to tell him about Mel. Since then, we've had a tenuous sort of peace between us, filled with stupid voice memos and out-of-context Snapchats, while I've been forced to text other friends to maintain some sort of social connection with people outside the house. It's not as fun, though.

I'm sending a text to Drew now as Dad ambles into the living room. With his unshaven face and sunken, tired eyes, he looks like an extra in a zombie movie, slow-moving and grunting in response to the barest questions. But he's freshly showered today, with an old-but-clean-looking Lakers jersey and a gentle smile. He gives me a kiss on the forehead and begins rummaging in the kitchen for breakfast.

I'm already on my third class of the day, and it's coming up on noon, so it's kind of late for breakfast, to be honest, but I know he's doing his best. He's a freelance music composer, so he doesn't have a typical nine-to-five job, meaning that with the "Mel situation," he could just be in bed all day. Instead, he's coming downstairs to spend time with me. He hasn't said that, but I know. There are like five TVs upstairs, and he's got his own "man cave" or whatever where he plays *Diablo* alone and *Overwatch* with his brothers in Indiana. Technically, he *could* be doing "research"—some of his clients are video game companies, after all. But most of the time, it sounds like he's just blasting stuff and threatening my uncles' dignity.

Today, like he's done for the last three days, he plops onto the couch in the living room, behind the kitchen island, with a bowl of cereal and turns on the TV.

At first, I hear sports commentators, and then I hear the news. The words seep into my brain before I can tune them out: *George Floyd. Choking. Police officers. Illegal hold.*

"You okay?" Dad calls from behind me, and I jerk around to look at him.

"What?" It sounds angrier than I mean it to.

"Are you okay? You sound like you're breathing hard."

"I'm fine," I say, but he peers closely at me, and that only makes me angrier. I know what he's thinking—or I think I do. Either I've caught the Covid virus that may or may not exist, or I'm about to have a mental breakdown like Mel.

Oh, did I leave that part out? Yeah, she's in the hospital because her girlfriend, Olivia, found her with a half-empty bottle of pills in her hand. Dad tried to convince Olivia to stay with us for a few days, to heal from the trauma, but she opted to stay home. Maybe she's got her own family or friends to help her out; I don't know. But what I do know is that whatever Mel is suffering from, it's what Alexis calls "a different kind of illness." I've heard that a lot of people don't know they have that either. It's another thing that lurks, which is why Dad is still observing me and pretending not to.

"Can you change the channel?" I ask.

He does—back to NBA reruns, since the playoffs are paused due to Covid this year—and I'm about to send Drew more hilarious memes about the end times when Alexis's smiling face breaks through my screen for a video call, along with the sound of birds chirping.

"Hiii, Tia," she says with the sort of cheeriness I assume comes from years of anti-anxiety medication.

"Hi," I say with far less enthusiasm. I haven't yet convinced Mom and Dad I'm old enough for crazy pills, as they jokingly call them, but maybe this year will do the trick.

"So . . . what are you up to?" she asks.

"Literally nothing."

"Aren't you in school right now?"

"'In school' is a very contentious term these days. Plus, it's the end of the semester, so there's not a lot of learning left. Most of our finals were this week."

"Right. Well." She takes a deep breath. "How are you feeling?" Of course, she must know how I'm feeling. It's probably not too different from how she's feeling.

"Fine," I say, and she sighs again, long and loud.

"Just fine?"

"I mean."

I can practically hear her shoulders rise and fall. "Yeah," she says, like she gets it, and I know she does. Our sister hasn't been awake in almost three days. I don't think either one of us is doing great. "I'm sorry I left," she says. "I'm going to try to come back in a few days."

I nod, though I'm not really upset. She got here as fast as she could when we found out about Mel, but her husband is out on a lighting job for a YouTube series and they fell prey to the most devious side effect of this "mysterious global illness": the pandemic puppy. Hers is a two-month-old smush-faced mutt who seems to hyperventilate as a matter of course, at least from the barrage of videos of him that Alexis has sent us. With everyone stuck at home, it turns out that the pandemic has been like Christmas for homeless dogs everywhere. Now they have doting human parents eager for yet another thing to worry over and spend money on.

I am not a fan. I don't know what it is—maybe I'm broken—but I have never understood the appeal. It's not just dogs, though. I'm an equal opportunity hater. Cats, ferrets, fish, mice, British geckos that sell car insurance. None of them make sense as housemates. All they do is eat, sleep, and cost money. I'm also, by the way, never having a kid. I question my parents' decision to have three.

Anyway, after freaking out over Mel with the rest of us, Alexis had to retrieve her dog from the friend who was babysitting him, so she's been back in San Diego for the last two days, picking up dog poop while I pretend like I care about even one of my classes. But then she asks something unexpected. "Do you want to come over?"

"I don't like drool," I tell her. It's a knee-jerk response.

"I know," she says, with obvious annoyance. "But since Houston is out of town for the YouTube shoot, the house is pretty empty, and it could be nice to hang out together. You know, some sisterly bonding."

Hmm. She only lives two hours away, so she usually comes to visit us and I haven't been to her new place yet. It might be a very welcome change of scenery.

As she continues to try to convince me of how cute and hip her neighborhood in North Hills is, another class with another final starts. I turn on my video, make sure it's muted, and prop my phone up on a water glass beside the computer so I can see Alexis at the same time. It all feels a little bit like white noise until the latest notification from Drew pops up.

There's a protest tonight, and I really think you should come. With everything going on with Mel, it might help you feel better.

You know that phrase *seeing red*? I don't think I've ever really understood it until now. I'm glaring so hard at my phone that Alexis stops talking to ask if she's upsetting me.

"No," I tell her. At the same time I text Drew:

Sorry. I'm going to San Diego tonight.

CHAPTER TWO

IT'S NIGHT BY THE TIME ALEXIS COMES TO THE house. The bright lights of her beige cruiser shine through the front windows. Dad opens the door before she has a chance to knock and then pulls her into a hug, all five feet ten inches of him seemingly wrapped around her like a willow tree.

When they pull away, Alexis touches his face. Her expression is a mirror of the concern he's been trying so hard to hide from me. With her, his mask of calm drops. Weariness drags down his cheeks instead, pulling his face like an anchor sinking to the bottom of a deep and treacherous ocean. In that moment, it's hard to tell who's the parent and who's the child.

"Hey," I say, and the scene resets. The mask settles

back on Dad's face and Alexis greets me by pulling one of the twists I painstakingly worked on during chemistry or history or something class a few days prior. Then she knocks me back with a crushing hug. Dad rubs his hands together, his eyes bright and animated as if he hasn't looked like the walking dead all day, and announces, "Dinner!" He plants a foot on the bottom step and calls up to Mom, who's been upstairs since last night, "Lisa! Alexis is here! Time to eat!"

A few minutes later, Mom meets us in the kitchen. "Thanks, Ray," she says to Dad. I resist the urge to shudder. Dad's name is Raymond. Everyone calls him Ray, except Mom. She says "babe" or "honey" or some sweet variation, but I've never heard her call him Ray, and the fact that she does so now makes my skin itch, like Mom's been occupied by some alien entity. She gives us both a tired kiss on the cheek before plopping into a chair at the table. Mom isn't like Dad. You can see the tearstains in the corner of her eyes, the set of her downturned lips, as if they'd never learned to smile quite right, even as she tries. Today, she's managed to put on hard pants and a non-pajama top, but she's still in the same bathrobe she's been wearing since we left Mel at the hospital. I don't know if she actually worked today either. Unlike Dad, Mom has a full-time job, translating movie and TV subtitles between English and Spanish, but I don't know if she took time off. All I know is that her office door was closed the entire day. All I know is that I haven't seen her.

When they see Mom, Alexis and Dad exchange a look, but they don't look at me, so I look at my phone and send the meme I'd been planning to share with Drew when Alexis first arrived. It's about *The Hunger Games*. We haven't talked since I told him I was going to San Diego tonight, but I don't want things to be awkward, yet again, so I'm hoping we can get back to talking about dumb stuff. Y'know, like dystopian nightmares.

Ha ha, he responds to the meme. Success.

I set my phone down as Dad puts the pizza he ordered on the table and hands Mom two slices of pepperoni. Alexis takes one slice of cheese and puts the salad she requested in a little bowl, and I take one slice of each.

"Ow," I shout, because I'm an idiot and forgot that hot cheese can scorch your taste buds.

"Don't hurt yourself," Mom chastises. Then, as if she said something particularly offensive, she sighs and buries her face in one hand. Her palm presses into her eye so hard I'm afraid *she's* going to hurt herself.

"How's the new puppy?" Dad asks Alexis. I'm grateful for the change of subject, and to soon be out of the house. Away from the heaviness that's settled into it like concrete and mold, somehow hard and creeping at the same time. The weight of it presses in on me; the stench of it feels suffocating. I can deal with a slobbering ball of fur for a few days if it means escaping all that.

"Adorable," Alexis responds with a gushing, sincere voice. "I'll show you pictures." She presses her phone screen into Mom's line of vision, and like a bright satellite against the fog, it seems to send Mom briefly back into her human skin.

"He's so cute, Alexis!" she coos, and soon they pull Dad into their warbling orbit of puppy pics and anecdotes. Alexis mumbles something about how loud Poirot can be sometimes—Pwa-roh, "like the Belgian detective," she reminds us, as if any of us know what she's talking about—and Mom launches into a story about how loud Alexis used to cry when she was a baby.

All good fun. Normal stuff. A tenuous sort of peace I could sink into, if I didn't know what was beneath the surface. As if one call from the hospital wouldn't send us all into a panicked frenzy. I pick up my phone again to send Drew a new text, when I see an alert come through.

New mask mandate in Orange County sparks anger, friction in restless city already racked with protests.

I groan, and my family stops mid-chatter to look at me. "Sorry," I mutter.

They exchange new looks with each other. The lack of subtlety is atrocious.

"I'm fine," I say. "Just tired of the news."

Alexis nods. "A lot's going on. My company announced a new diversity initiative in response to George Floyd. Says they're aiming to increase diversity by fifty percent in my department."

Dad snorts. "So, there will be *two* Black project managers, instead of one?"

"Yup. On a team of twenty."

Dad lifts his pizza in a kind of salute. "Progress."

I hate when they talk like this. Not because they're wrong, but because it makes me feel even more tired and helpless. Like, there's all this talk of change and growth and how far the world has come with things like racism, and then you turn on the news, or go to work, or look around the dinner table, and realize everyone is still exhausted and traumatized. The world is starved of justice, and we're getting by on crumbs.

No wonder Mel tried to nope out.

The thought comes before I can knock it away. Mel. My sister, the only person missing from the table right now, and missing *by choice*. Suddenly, her absence is so heavy that my chest feels like it'll be crushed by the weight of it. I try to control my breathing, so I don't get those looks of worry that my family is terrible at hiding, and when I can't, I excuse myself to the bathroom instead. Splash water on my face. Press my forehead to the mirror. Double-check that my twists are still twisted. I feel like a shell of a person, but I'd rather not *look* like it.

When I finally pull feeling back into my body, I return to the table, where it looks like dinner is coming to an end. Alexis asks if I'm ready to go, and it takes every shred of willpower I have not to race toward the door. I don't want to spend another second watching the shadow of joy I saw on Mom's face slide back into oblivion.

Once we've said our goodbyes, I throw my stuff into Alexis's back seat and knock the front seat so far back that I'm nearly lying down by the time the engine turns. Immediately, Utada Hikaru blares through the speakers. Alexis has been on an Utada kick ever since the pandemic started back in March—she says it reminds her of simpler times, when she was in high school playing *Kingdom Hearts* for the first time; or sometimes, it just helps her imagine being somewhere else. The idea that high school is "simpler times" makes me want to weep, but I get wanting to be somewhere else. To imagine there's someplace outside your city, or your country. Someplace you could belong. Or be safe. Or even just a little bit sane.

I listen to Utada's voice and attempt to pick out the few Japanese words Alexis has taught me. When that fails, I take out my phone and scroll through messages from a few other friends, but they're all asking me how Mel is, and if I'm doing okay; I don't have the energy to be honest, and I don't have the energy to lie, so I don't respond at all. Not even to my friend Robbie, who's one of the few classmates Drew and I have hung out with this semester. That was before my sisters finally convinced our parents that the pandemic is real; at least real enough for us to avoid interactions outside of our "quarantine bubble," or whatever. Drew was part of that bubble, though. Until now.

So, I let the music take me away and try to think about what *my* simpler time would be. Definitely before the pandemic. Or before George Floyd was killed and Drew decided he wanted to reignite the Black Panther Party. Or before Mel took too many pills and left my parents shell-shocked like the survivors of a sudden deadly storm.

Or, or, or.

I guess "simpler" can't be very clearly defined.

What I do know is that a lot can change in the span of a few months. That six months ago, my biggest worries were senioritis, college applications, and whether I had a crush on Drew. I could say we've been friends forever and a day, but that's just because we've been in the same orbit since we were in elementary school. We saw each other around. My friends played with his friends. We got older, got closer, discovered similar interests, like listening to musical soundtracks on repeat and seeing how long it would take for our parents to beg us to stop belting Barbra Streisand ballads.

Drew came out to me in the eighth grade. He told me about a boy who'd drawn him a special Valentine's Day card with a chibi version of the two of them holding hands. Drew had thrown it away and told the boy to leave him alone. That *I* was his girlfriend, which was, obviously, news to me. Then, as we sat in his living room, listening to "Seasons of Love" on the *Rent* movie soundtrack, Drew pulled his knees up, ashy brown skin pressed against the holes of his black jeans, black finger-coils falling into his deep brown eyes. He bent his head down, whispered a question into his skin. *What if I wanted to be his valentine?* He wouldn't look at me when I grabbed his hand and said, "Of course you do, stupid. He's cute!"

What I hadn't told Drew that night was that I was thinking the same thing of him—that maybe I wanted to be *his* valentine. That maybe *we* could be valentines. But over the last few years, I've wavered on whether that was even true. Did I *love* Drew or was I *in love* with

Drew? And if I *was* in love with Drew, why did I never seem interested in any other boys?

I didn't swoon when Alexis showed me pictures of the hot K-pop groups she followed or when Mom put on classic Hollywood movies and said, "Now HE's fine." Both EXO's Kai and a young Denzel Washington—or even a seasoned one—were indeed good-looking, but those were just objective facts. It wasn't until Alexis showed me a music video with Amber Liu that an objective fact became personal preference. Amber wasn't just hot, she was . . . I mean. Have you *seen* her?

But then there was Drew. My Drew, sweet and sensitive and kind of gangly until we hit sixteen in tenth grade, and he hit the gym, and all of a sudden he was . . . well. Not gangly. Very much not. He had muscles, and cheekbones, and still knew every word to the *Hamilton* soundtrack.

And it was *Hamilton* that led to every debilitating change that's happened since.

So, another night. This time, we're outside, and the sky is a spill of ink with spots of stars that blink in and out of time like the beat of my heart. Drew and I are lying next to each other on a blanket in his yard, shoulders and forearms and wrists touching, skin bare and clothed, bodies warm, and voices raw.

Raw, because we've been singing "Satisfied" on

repeat. The song where Angelica Schuyler introduces Alexander Hamilton to her sister Eliza and then immediately regrets it.

"Romance is tragic," Drew says, when we finally exhaust our lungs. "Like, Hamilton is genuinely in love with Eliza, right, but also so clearly in love with Angelica."

"Right," I say. "And at the same time, Angelica is married, later, and we know from 'Congratulations' that she didn't really love her husband. But she definitely loved Hamilton. But, like, she also loves and adores and respects her sister. So, it's a quagmire."

"Totally," he says.

That's the kind of stuff we always end up talking about. On any given night, we could be lying on opposite ends of his twin bed, letting the music play as we philosophize about love, and life, and the state of the world. You know. Normal teen stuff.

But that night, when our words stilled, he turned his face to me. Brown eyes now hazel in the light of the moon, they filled with . . . I don't know. *Something.* Something electric.

I don't know who kissed who first. I can't tell you if I took off his shirt, or if he took off my bra. All I know is that ten minutes later, I was fully dressed and bounding up the stairs of my own house, not caring if my parents awoke to my sobbing. They didn't hear me, though. And I pretended not to hear my phone the first fifteen times Drew called, until I finally turned it on silent. We didn't speak for the rest of that week. Or the week after. Before the protest. Before Mel. In simpler times, it was a kiss that turned our unbreakable bond brittle.

"Hey, Alexis?" I say, finally turning my attention back to the car ride.

"Mm?"

"Can I tell you something?"

Alexis nods without taking her eyes off the road and turns the music down. For some reason, the lack of sound suddenly makes me feel colder. I reach forward and turn up the heat. She doesn't stop me. As my bones thaw, I take a deep breath and focus on the Totoro air freshener that dangles from her rearview mirror. It must have lost its scent a long time ago, because the car smells only like dust and hot air, but I feel calmer, nonetheless.

"So . . . Drew and I kissed." I say the words slowly, feeling them out. It's the first time I've said them out loud and not in text.

Alexis blinks once. Twice. "Oh."

"Well . . . we . . . slightly more than kissed. But less than sexed."

She lets out a long, deep breath. Alexis and I have

talked about sex before, in a clinical, feminist, your-body-is-your-own type of way. But I've never actually talked to her about my own sexual activity. I imagine she's having a small panic attack right now despite the meds. BABY SISTER HAVING SEX. BABY SISTER HAVE SEX. WHAT DO. WHAT DO.

A car honks at us aggressively; Alexis has apparently slowed down too much in the carpool lane. She clears her throat. Shakes out her shoulders. Takes another quick glance my way as the car that honked switches lanes and then pulls in front of us. "Okay," she says. "And . . . how was that for you two?"

"I don't know," I say, sinking into my seat.

"Okay," she says again. "Are you okay?"

"I don't know."

"Did he hurt you?"

"No, not at all."

"Okay."

She waits for me to continue, as the white lights of passing cars dance across her face. Finally, I manage a cohesive sentence. "Drew is . . . not straight."

"Yes." She nods affirmatively, as if it's the first thing I've said in English.

"But I thought that he was like . . . absolutely not straight."

"Mm-hmm."

"Whereas it seems like he's maybe possibly like . . . kind of straight."

"You mean, bisexual?"

"Yes. I mean, that's actually what he told me, after."

Alexis taps her fingers on the wheel for a moment as the car comes to a slow crawl. It looks like traffic has picked up, and now we're barely moving. "Okay," she says again. "So, what's the problem?"

"Oh." I shrug nonchalantly. "Nothing. It's just . . . I think, like, *I* might be gay."

Alexis doesn't bat an eye. "Ah," she says. "And you didn't know before?"

"I wasn't sure."

"Mm-hmm. And you don't think you can tell Drew?"

"What am I supposed to tell him? *Hey, I know you're my best friend, and we made out, and kissing made you realize that you're bi, but it actually made me realize that I'm gay. Sorry!*"

Alexis tries valiantly not to laugh. She clears her throat instead. "How do you know you're gay, and not just, like, not attracted to Drew?"

"Because Drew is the only guy I've ever seriously thought I *was* attracted to." I sigh. "And it turns out that . . . I'm not."

"Ah," she says again. "Well."

I can tell she's thinking about the right thing to say,

and I don't blame her, because it's not like there's really a playbook for this sort of thing. Mel would probably be better suited to talking about this, given that she, too, is a raging homosexual, but she is otherwise occupied. By a hospital bed and an IV needle. I did text her about it, though. Before I found out what happened.

The cars ahead of us begin to move, and our car picks up speed again. Soon, a highway sign for San Diego appears, and Alexis turns off the music. The radio comes on: Two disc jockeys are in the middle of ribbing each other. We catch the end of a joke, in time to hear a young woman laugh, "*Ha ha, you think you're so funny, Joe.*"

"*Speaking of funny,*" Joe says, "*What do you think about that audio that was leaked from Councilman Lowry?*"

"*Oof,*" the woman responds. "*I don't know if I'd call that funny. It's harsh.*"

"*Well, what he said was harsh—*"

Another young woman cuts in, "*Wait, I didn't hear about this; what did he say?*"

"*Mags,*" Joe admonishes. "*Where have you been? There are so many jokes about it on social right now. You've seen it, Tay.*"

"*Yeah, it's even got its own viral dance,*" Tay says.

"*Okay, okay, fine, but what did the councilman say?*" Mags responds.

"Councilman Lowry called the recent Black Lives Matter protests 'un-American,' and those protesters nothing but 'thugs' and 'opportunists.'"

"*Ooh*," Mags groans. "*Bleak*."

"*Yeah*," Joe says, "*the audio has been remixed a bunch of times, usually with something from NWA or Tupac's classic anthem, 'Trapped.'*"

Alexis scoffs as I hit my head against the seat. "And yet the protests against masking and quarantining are totally fine?" she says. "Is he serious?"

"Can we turn it off?" I ask.

Alexis sighs and snaps off the radio. Utada comes back to us. "Sorry," she says. "I like the local station—the hosts are usually pretty funny. But our councilman is an absolute racist piece of shit. I even voted for him, before I found out that he was a lying sack of—"

"Mm-hmm," I say, and hope she takes the hint. She does, and we lapse back into silence as we pass billboards for LEGOLAND and the San Diego Botanic Garden.

I *could* tell my sister about the other thing. That Drew and I had managed to move past The Awkward Thing, before The Deadly Thing, and now he's pissed at me because I'm not an incredible outspoken Black activist like Angela Davis. Although, she, too, is gay. Maybe it would cancel it out if I tell him I'm at least one of those things. Maybe he'd feel better if I was closer to something he recognized. Someone he trusted.

"Alexis," I start again. I swallow, then find my courage. "Is it hard for you, with Houston being white and everything?" It's the closest thing I can think of to my current predicament. Alexis takes a sharp inhale, like the question about her white husband is a gut punch. I wonder if she's gotten a lot of questions like that. "I mean, right now," I try to amend. "With, you know, everything . . ."

"I understand," she says gently. "I mean, I think it would be harder if Houston were a different person. Or, I don't know, maybe if I was. If we didn't know how to talk to each other and support each other." She taps her fingers on the wheel again. I look out the window, but there's not much to see in the dark mass of the evening. "Race affects absolutely everything," Alexis starts again slowly. "And also . . . I'm an individual. So is Houston. And there are so many things we can connect on, and that we love each other for . . ." She blinks up at the ceiling of the car and then back at the road, searching for the words. "Houston couldn't care less about anime, for example, and I couldn't tell you one thing about YouTube culture that he hasn't told me first. But we listen when we talk about the things we care about, and we *know* what each other cares about. And we love a lot of the same things, like art museums and mystery shows. On our first date, we stayed up until two in the morning talking about religion and science because we found out we both love *Contact* by Carl Sagan." She pauses, takes another breath.

"If Houston didn't understand the different power dynamics at play in the world, because he's white and a man, and I'm Black and a woman, and therefore how that works in our relationship . . . if he couldn't see those things, especially this week, with George Floyd, it would . . . oh, it would suck. I probably couldn't even look at him. But then, I also probably wouldn't have married him. This week, he has stepped up as my partner and offered comfort when I needed it, and that . . ." She sighs. "It makes a big difference. It makes a huge difference that he understands what happened–what's happening, and why, and why it affects me differently than it affects him, even if it enrages him too. So, yeah." She shrugs. "He gets it."

Yeah. That does sound like the Houston I know. I suppose I could've guessed the answer to my own question then, but people can surprise you. Mom and Dad always say that. Maybe I've surprised Drew. Maybe I've let him think I'm a stronger person than I am, and now . . . well, now I've shown him the real me.

And that really sucks.

So, I sink into the ride as more road signs and billboards and cars pass. Quietly, Alexis starts to sing, her voice a gentle complement to Utada's lyrics, and I wonder back to that night beneath the stars, when Drew and I taught each other deeper truths about ourselves than we would've found out on our own. I think about Hamilton, and Angelica, and Eliza, and the ways they seemed to love each other so genuinely and completely, even when it hurt. Even when it made everything else that much harder, murkier, uncertain. At least in Lin-Manuel Miranda's retelling, that kind of love seems so real, so tangible. But was it really possible—especially in the middle of a war? One has to wonder:

How can love seem so abundant when everything else is dying?

CHAPTER THREE

WHEN WE GET TO ALEXIS'S PLACE TWENTY minutes later, she throws her seatbelt off then sprints up the stairs to her second-floor apartment. I barely have time to follow her through the gate of her small complex and past her front door as she hurries over to Poirot's kennel and unlatches the lock.

A tiny mass of short, light brown fur and skinny legs propels itself through the air, accompanied by a high-pitched puppy bark as Poirot yelps in joy. His pointy, black-tipped ears are pulled so far back that they're pinned to the back of his little head, and his small pink tongue attacks every inch of Alexis's skin it can reach, which Alexis, to her credit, tries to keep from her face. Instead, she presses her cheek to the side of his squirmy belly and apologizes for how long she was out. “It’s okay, my sweet little baby, it’s okay,” she coos. She risks a quick nuzzle to his smushed black snout, dodging his tongue again as I pretend not to gag. Then I step farther into her apartment.

“Whoa,” I say. “It smells awful in here.”

“I know,” she says apologetically. “He’s still learning to hold it, and I was gone for a while.” She inspects Poirot’s butt and paws as if he were a newborn human child, even as his long, skinny tail whips around wildly in excitement. Apparently satisfied that he’s not covered in his own poop, she plops him back on the ground and hurries to the kitchen. “Just gotta clean this up,” she says, “and then I’ll spray the house.”

She hurries between his kennel by the front door and the bathroom at the back of the apartment, while I reconsider my decision to stay with her for the weekend. Poirot sniffs my shoes and I lift up my feet and step back. I need to be wary of falling prey to whatever curse he’s cast on my sister, lest I, too, become a maidservant to the fur prince.

“Okay,” Alexis says finally, huffing as she wipes her forehead. “All done. I just have to take him out.”

“But he already went,” I tell her, in case she’s forgotten the last ten minutes. I wonder if baby brain applies to dog moms.

"Yeah," she says. "But it's part of his training. So, even though he's already gone, he's got to get used to the routine of going out when I get home, so that eventually he learns that I *will* come home to let him out, and then he learns to hold it."

"Sure," I say, because whatever. Why not just get a chia pet? I'm pretty sure they don't leave your house smelling like feces.

"Cool," she says, and then hesitates. "Wait. It's Friday night. I have to take out the trash too."

"Right now?"

"Yeah. Trash day is tomorrow. They come at, like, seven A.M." She sighs, and for a split second, my usually calm and collected big sister looks like she might become a complete and total wreck. "Okay. First, I'll take out Poirot, and then I'll take out the trash, and then—"

"Where does the trash go?" I cut in. I can't take this level of logistics at ten thirty at night.

"Downstairs," she says, looking at me like I've just shown her the elixir of life. "Just behind the building."

As she outfits Poirot with a tiny black-and-gold harness, I consolidate the trash from her kitchen and bathroom and trudge back outside. I'm not usually so helpful, but I hate seeing Alexis look so . . . lost. It was only a split second, but the idea that she, too, might have the ability to break gives me a deep and probing terror. I don't want to imagine it. Not again.

Once outside, the dumpster is easy to find. It's in the alleyway behind the apartment complex, just like Alexis told me. It's not pitch-black outside; the surrounding complexes have lights and I can see down one end of the alleyway that there's a bar still open. The chances of me getting kidnapped are relatively low, though I suspect they're higher than if I was still at home in the suburbs. For the second time tonight, I question my decision to leave the relative safety of Irvine. It's only the memory of my parents' haunted faces and Alexis's own tired expression that keeps me from seeking an early-morning retrieval.

Still, I realize I should probably tell my parents we made it to San Diego. I walk back through the rear door of the complex and lean against one of the walls of the small entryway as I dial Mom's number. She answers on the first ring.

"Hi, baby," she says. She doesn't sound like she's in bed, meaning she was probably waiting up to hear from me. "You get there okay?"

"Yeah. How's Dad?"

"Telling Josiah to watch his six," Mom says. That means Dad is shooting digital people in his office and cheering about it with his boys. Honestly, kind of ironic. Except, you know. Those people aren't real.

"Cool. Well, I'm going back upstairs. I just took the trash out for Alexis."

"That's nice of you, honey. I'll let your father know you called. Oh, and Tia?"

"Yeah?"

"You and your sister take care of each other, okay?"

It's a simple request. Something she would say, probably something she *has* said, at one point or another. And yet . . .

"We will," I whisper. I hold the words like a frail and frightened thing. Not too firmly or they'll dissipate in the wind.

We hang up and I heave myself off the wall, suddenly exhausted as I walk back toward Alexis's place. It's one of just four apartments in the complex: two buildings, which are situated in a semicircle around a small courtyard that leads to the front exit and onto the main street that we parked at. The stairs to her place are in the middle, serving as a sort of grand, curving decoration that separates the front building from the back.

When I reach the bottom of the stairs, I glance toward the apartment beneath Alexis's and nearly jump back in surprise. There's a figure sitting on the bench in front of it. I don't want to stare too hard at a stranger, but his face isn't what grabs me anyway. It's the birds. One on the left shoulder with green and yellow feathers, almost glowing in the fluorescent light above the apartment door and bobbing its head up and down as if agreeing to whatever the man is saying. The other bird, on the right shoulder, is slightly bigger than the first, with a blue chest and darker feathers on its back. It's shuffling, slowly, side to side, listless but also, apparently, listening. I take a few steps back and slip around the thick brick exterior of the stairs, making sure the person between the birds can't see me behind the pink facade. Then I hear a low, gravelly voice.

"Well, Mr. Bastion, I don't know what to say about the news today. That Gavin Newsom is a real piece of work." The figure then clears his throat and adopts a higher pitch. "I mean, maybe the governor's on to something. After all, the *plan*demic really is working according to PLAN."

What the hell?

"Plan," one of the birds chirps back. "Plan!"

I speed up the stairs and shut the door behind me. I'm pacing when Alexis finally returns with Poirot a few minutes later. When she sees me, her pale brown face turns into an eerie sort of white.

"What is it? What's wrong?"

"What's wrong?" I exclaim, throwing my hands in the air. "What's wrong? Bruh! Who is that man downstairs talking to his birds like Norman freaking Bates?"

"Oh." Alexis gives me a look like I'm the one being ridiculous as she kicks off her shoes and reaches for the wipes she keeps by the door entrance. "That's just Parakeet Man. Don't pay him any mind; he's harmless," she says. Then she begins cleaning each of Poirot's feet.

The look I give her suggests that she might have two more heads than she realized. "Are you kidding? He was just debating whether the liberals have concocted a murderous worldwide viral infection for some unknown plan." I've heard the conspiracy from various protests and news articles since the shutdown in March—it wasn't hard to extrapolate the argument "Parakeet Man" was having. Alone. "He was conversing with himself, by the way. Through the birds." I feel Alexis needs this crucial piece of information.

"It's fine," she says breezily. She releases Poirot from his harness and then gives him eight hundred kisses on his head as he tries desperately to lick her face again. Thankfully, she still doesn't let him. "I've lived here for almost two years," she says. "I think he's been here much longer than that. He's a little eccentric, and kind of rude, but otherwise, it's never been a problem. Don't worry." She rubs her face thoughtfully. "He *did* pass out a bunch of flyers about masks being a form of mind control, but that just tells me he's concerned for our collective well-being."

"That's terrifying–and also counterintuitive."

"Well." She shrugs, and I want to throttle her.

When Poirot remembers he has a tail and starts to chase it, Alexis puts her hands on her hips and looks around like she's seeing her apartment for the first time. "Okay," she says. "Let me show you around."

I am not exactly fond of this change of subject, but Mom asked us to take care of each other, so I guess I have to do my part and let it go. For now.

Anyway, it's a nice place: a little one bedroom with a living room and two large windows that look out onto the complex and its neighbors; a small functional kitchen through an archway to the left; and Alexis and Houston's bedroom behind us, through a short hallway that's more like a nook in the wall, separating it from the bathroom that's across from the bedroom door.

There are also very nice leafy plants throughout the living room and kitchen that I would definitely kill, but of course Alexis keeps them lively and green. I'm informed that I must hold the toilet handle down for a count of five seconds, and also that there are a handful of coffee shops right around the corner that have makeshift outdoor setups, if I feel like venturing out into the world. Alexis knows I hate coffee, but the idea of being able to see people that don't just exist on a screen *does* make my heart skip a beat.

When she's done showing me the basics, I take up residence on the pullout couch in the living room while Alexis gets ready for sleep in her bedroom. As I stare up at the ceiling, my current situation dawns on me. How exactly did I end up with springs digging into my back in the room next to a stinky dog and above a parakeet hoarder, in the middle of a pandemic, a racial uprising, and the potential collapse of my friendship due the possibility that I bat for the sapphic team?

It kind of feels like a lot.

I take out my phone and fully draft an entire text before I remember that Mel, who usually bears the brunt of my midnight musings, can't read it. Right. How could I forget? I delete the message, and then consider deleting my contacts, my social media, and every picture I've ever taken–like a sudden and necessary cleanse. For a second, it almost makes sense. For a second, I think I can understand that desire to disappear, quickly, cleanly, as if you were never there to begin with.

"Hello?" I hear Alexis's voice from her bedroom. I

figure it must be her husband, Houston, until I catch the next few words.

". . . Still monitoring . . . ? Yes . . . Have you talked to . . . ?"

I press my ear closer to the wall, but I can't make out much more than that. Alexis must be walking around the room. But I know she's talking to either Mom or Olivia. I know Mel isn't awake yet, or else we'd already be on our way back to Irvine. Instead, we're here, wondering what's going to happen next, and if we're ready to face it.

INTERLUDE #1

I WAS SEVEN THE FIRST TIME MEL WENT TO THE hospital. She was nineteen.

That time, she hadn't tried to hurt herself yet, but we thought she was going to. Or, well, Mom, Dad, and Alexis thought she was. I was too young to really understand what was going on. All I knew was that Mel was "hurt," and we had to take care of her.

I remember going to the psychiatric campus she was at, which was different than a typical hospital. Since it was years before the pandemic, we were all allowed to visit, so we sat in this tiny reception-like room while Mel picked out colored pencils. She was flipping through a coloring book like the ones we had at school. Hers had a bunch of pretty images from nature, more sophisticated than the line drawings of Disney characters that I was used to at the time. After a few minutes of silent flipping, Mel landed on a detailed outline of a conch shell. She pressed the blunted end of the colored pencil she chose onto the black lines and followed each swirl and curve, until the black was mirrored in gold.

After a moment, Alexis stood up and moved to sit next to her. "Can I help?"

Mel just nodded, and Alexis reached for an emerald-green pencil. She started on one side while Mel colored the other. Their shoulders touched as their hands moved, the two of them working in tandem. Dad watched until his rigid broad shoulders suddenly went slack. His large brown hands covered his face, and I heard what I thought sounded like crying. I couldn't be sure, though, because he stood up almost immediately and walked out the door.

I was sitting in Mom's lap and she whispered in my ear that everything would be okay, except that I didn't understand why it wasn't already okay. No one really explained anything to me, until later that night, when Alexis took me aside. Mel was still at the hospital.

"Is Mel okay?" I asked.

Alexis hesitated and then bent down to my level. "Mel is a little stressed. So am I," she said. "It happens to the best of us. That's why we both take medication.

It's okay. It's just that sometimes, some of us become more stressed than others, for different reasons. And sometimes, that means that we need a little more help than usual."

It was a convoluted way of saying Mel had depression. She stayed in the hospital for a couple more days, and then she came home. That was it.

There have been other scares since, but nothing like this—with the pills, and the induced coma. We've always been afraid of what she might do, but I don't think any of us really thought . . . at least, we didn't expect it. Not this time. After all, she's been doing really well. She has a good job in marketing or something. She and her girlfriend, Olivia, have been together since their second year of college. She seemed pretty happy, all things considered.

And then?

Well, like Alexis said, we all get stressed for different reasons. There's a mysterious disease, worldwide quarantines, and then you watch a man who looks like your father get murdered, repeatedly, on different national news networks.

Some people bend. And others . . .

I guess sometimes they break.

TEXT MESSAGE #1

(OR WHAT I WOULD HAVE TEXTED MEL IF SHE WERE AWAKE)

Hiii, this week has been insane. I'm exhausted, and Alexis's pullout couch sucks. Also, I'm kind of worried about her. She seems fine—but, like, she always seems fine. And you seemed fine, before you weren't. And Drew and I are talking again, after the uh . . . well, I told you about that. But now he seems upset that I'm not gung-ho on going to protests or writing memos to the school board or doing all the things that seem to come naturally to him. He thinks I don't care. And I do. I swear I do. But, Mel, I'm so tired, all the time. ALL the time. And now I'm scared that I'm not who he wants me to be. I'm not a straight girl, and I'm pretty sure I'm not bi, and now I'm not "woke" or "woke enough," or whatever either. I feel like I'm failing him. I feel like I'm failing you too. Because we talk all the time, and I didn't know. I didn't know you weren't okay, Mel, and now I don't know if you'll ever be okay again. What did I miss? Why didn't you say anything? Why didn't you tell me? What didn't you tell me?

Okay . . .

I think that's all.

Good night. I love you.

CHAPTER FOUR

IN THE MORNING, ALEXIS GOES TO MAKE US breakfast and promptly realizes that she's out of eggs, bread, fruit, vegetables, cereal, or anything a rational human being would consider food. Not even a single frozen meal. This would be funny, if not for the fact that this is very unlike Alexis. My calm, cool, and collected, put-together, has-a-plan-for-everything sister having a nearly empty fridge, except for Poirot's wet dog food is . . . alarming. One more thing that is completely out of the norm.

"Sorry," she says with a sigh. "Houston's been the one getting food since everything shut down in March, and I forgot to go out before you got here."

"Why did he leave you here anyway?" I blurt before I can stop myself.

Alexis rolls her eyes. “Because we need to pay our rent, and his job needs him on-site in the middle of a global pandemic because capitalism hates us all.” Then she takes another deep breath. “I’ll go out,” she says, and dons a paper mask before I can think to suggest takeout. “It’ll take a while since the grocery stores are . . .”

“A hellscape?”

“Yeah, that. But it shouldn’t be more than an hour, if I try a smaller mom-and-pop store a couple neighborhoods over. Houston told me that folks haven’t found out about that one yet.”

If that’s not depressingly apocalyptic, I don’t know what is, but neither of us wants to acknowledge it. I’m about to offer to go with her, when she points to Poirot, who is currently trying to bite the light beam that’s streaming in through the partially opened blinds of the living room.

“Can you watch that one?” she asks.

I stare at him and ponder how it’s possible for something so ridiculous to be able to survive. But I guess that’s why puppies have owners. Er, or parents. Whatever. “Sure,” I say. “What do I have to do?”

The answer is, apparently, very long, but the gist is to make sure he uses the bathroom outside and doesn’t otherwise hurt himself by eating the baseboards or licking the electric sockets or doing other things most creatures know will kill you.

"He's a baby," Alexis reminds me.

"Yeah, yeah," I say, and then she's out the door, imbuing me with a kind of trust I'm not entirely sure I deserve.

For the first minute or two, Poirot continues biting the light beam. But then he looks around. He sniffs the floor, goes to sniff the kitchen. The bathroom. Alexis's room. When he realizes she's gone, he stumbles to the door—his paws *do* seem disproportionately large for his body—and lets out the most ungodly sound I've ever heard in my life, like a banshee who's been smoking since birth. He scratches at the door with desperation, his cries getting louder and ever more mournful with each passing second.

I remember Alexis telling my parents that Poirot can be a little loud, but this is not loud. This is the sound of the earth rupturing as demons ascend from Hades. "Dude, can you . . ." I grab my phone from the counter as Poirot continues screaming. "It's okay, dude—bud. It's . . . *oh my God.*" Now I'm trying to call Alexis, but the phone keeps going to voicemail, and Poirot keeps screaming, and I have absolutely no idea what to do except keep dialing her number, until I—somehow—hear a banging on the door that surpasses even Poirot's howls.

"Yeah, just . . . one second." I drop my phone and look around desperately. Then it strikes me that maybe I can stop Poirot from screaming if I just shove something in his mouth. I speed-walk to the kitchen and reach for the treats Alexis told me about, while whoever is at the door continues to bang. "Here, Poirot. Here, boy." The sight of me in the kitchen seems to bring him back to his senses and he trots over to me—tongue lolling, tail wagging—as if he hadn't just been screaming his head off. He gobbles down three doggie bacon strips and then wobbles as he sits down, like it's something he just learned how to do, and stares up at me expectantly. "Good boy," I tell him.

But I'm lying. He is *not* a good boy.

The banging on the door continues. "Stay," I say to Poirot, which he ignores completely. He follows, nipping at my ankles, and I pick him up with a huff, before finally opening the front door. In front of me is a tall, rail-thin, sallow-faced white man with gray-green eyes and long, wiry white hair curling in his nostrils. His head is also covered in wiry white hair, but he's so tall that his nostrils are all I can seem to focus on—especially since he's looking down at me.

"Your dog," he says in a deep, mournful voice, "is disturbing my parakeets." He looks toward Poirot with a sneer.

Ah. So, *this* is Parakeet Man. Nice to know he's even more unsettling up close. I'd love to slam the door in his face, but Alexis claims—however dubiously—that they've never had serious problems before, so I'd rather not crash that streak. Instead, I try to conjure the sort of charming grin I've seen Mel give to store clerks the rare times she's a few cents short for a purchase. "Sorry," I say. "Won't happen again." Obviously, though, this is also a lie. If he's been here as long as Poirot has, Parakeet Man probably knows it too.

He blinks at me again and then turns around slowly, and I imagine his bones creaking like unoiled hinges. He takes one long stride after another back toward the stairs that lead down to the first floor, his bobbing head incongruous with his long, lanky figure. He disappears from my sight and I close the door, a huge sigh escaping my lungs. Between whatever banshee possessed Poirot and whatever ghoul is possessing *that* dude, I don't know if I'm feeling relief or just the beginning stages of panic.

I am going to *kill* Alexis.

"It's not that bad," she says when she finally calls me, in response to all of the rageful text messages I've sent her over the last ten minutes.

"Oh, I beggeth to differ, dear sister."

"Okay, fine," she says. "Really. Poirot has actually gotten so much better with his crying, but you're new so maybe he regressed. I genuinely didn't think he'd be that bad."

"Sure. And what about Count Olaf downstairs?"

"I told you he's fine."

"He's terrifying."

"He's . . . definitely not the most welcoming person. But all he ever does is complain about Poirot, and before we had him, we only ever heard the parakeets. Which, by the way, wake us up. Every. Single. Morning . . . since we moved in. So, he can deal with Poirot."

"How many parakeets does he have?"

"Too many."

Awesome. At least the parakeets didn't wake *me* up. It must be easier to hear them from her room. After she assures me, again, that Parakeet Man will be mostly harmless, I hang up and look at Poirot, wondering how the hell I'm going to deal with him for the next hour on my own. My phone buzzes again, and thinking it's Alexis, I mindlessly swipe to answer, failing to register in time the telltale *hee-haw* of an enthusiastic donkey.

"Hey," Drew says, and I nearly drop the phone.

"Hi," I say, knowing my voice is entirely too high.

Still, he laughs, and the familiar sound gives me a small sense of comfort. "What are you up to?"

"Oh my God," I say. "I have to tell you about this morning." I launch into a play-by-play of Poirot and Parakeet Man, and by the end we're both laughing so hard that I forget why, exactly, things have been so weird between us.

"I miss you." He sighs, and it makes me feel warm and gooey inside, because, right, yes, this is my best friend! And we love each other! How wonderful!

"I miss you too," I say.

"So, have you read the news lately?" he asks, and then I remember that we are actually in the worst timeline.

"No," I say. That's it. Just *no.*

"Okay," he says. "I mean, that's cool. It's just— remember that action we were planning at the school? The one I told you about?"

"Yeah."

"Well, I guess somebody told somebody, and now there's like an article about it on the *OC Register*. They interviewed school officials and everything, and they're trying to shut down any 'unsanctioned' school activity."

"Okay."

"Yeah," he says. He's quiet for a minute, but I don't fill the silence. I hear shuffling on his end of the phone, and I can imagine him running his hand through his curls, biting his lip. Actions I thought were sexy, but now I realize were just *him*—the things I love about him, as much as I love singing show tunes together and camping outside in safe and shielded environs. "How's Mel?" he asks finally.

I try to perk up a little more at this, because at least it's chaos I feel slightly more connected to. Even though the answer is still "I don't know."

"I'm sorry, man," he says. "Is Alexis good?"

And to that, the answer remains "I don't know." I tell him about the breakfast fiasco this morning, and he clucks his tongue.

"That's not like her."

"I know," I say. "I think she's more stressed than usual with Houston gone too," I add, thinking back to our conversation in the car. "Like, he grounds her a lot, I think, and with everything going on . . . what if it's another Mel situation? We think she's good, but this is just the first sign that, like, something is up. Maybe she needs help."

"Because of the pandemic? Or because of Mel?"

Or because of everything. *I don't know.*

Suddenly, I don't want to talk about this anymore either. "I gotta go," I say. "I—gah. Dammit! Poirot!" I don't mean to shout, but Poirot is now doing his business in the hallway instead of the puppy pad by the door. "I really do have to go. Puppy duty. Literally." Drew barely gets out an "I'll text you later," before I've let my phone drop and am racing toward Poirot to bring his squat, hunched body over to the door. Then I saddle him up as Alexis instructed and lead him to the outside world.

Let no one ever say that I am a bad sister.

At the last second, I run back in to grab a mask since Alexis informed me earlier that it's not so much a suggestion here, like in Irvine, as it is a standard expectation. I'll have to get used to that. Then we hurry past Parakeet Man's door and out of the complex, and Poirot begins sniffing like he's attempting to solve a mystery.

We walk, and since I have no destination in mind, I take the opportunity to look around. Most of what I'd seen the night before was a dark alleyway, a dumpster, and a bird-wielding nightmare. But in the daylight, the neighborhood is warm, colorful, and bustling with activity, even as people—mostly white, but occasionally not—don their masks and stay the requisite six feet away from one another. Still, they smile at Poirot and nod pleasantly in my direction. A couple folks even hold back barely concealed squeals at seeing a puppy out and about, like it's the most precious thing in the world.

Soon, we leave my sister's street and pass into a more commercial area. There are shops that look like they've been there for decades: not dilapidated or unkempt, but certainly well-worn, and distinct from one another. Some are tiny, blink-and-you-miss-it holes-in-the-wall with funky chalkboard signs urging you to enter. Others look like they could be cute bungalows that once belonged to small families, but now they're coffee shops, as denoted by the myriad picnic tables in the front yards, or an old theater that now houses a different coffee shop, a record store, and an art gallery.

I pull Poirot from a piece of chicken bone that missed the trash can outside a concert venue, but when we get to the stop sign at the end of the street, I don't see the melted vanilla ice cream cone fast enough to keep him from gobbling it down. I glower at him, but he doesn't notice, and why should he? It is an indisputable fact that ice cream is delicious—probably more so if it's covered in dirt and trash, if you're a dog. I don't know. We keep walking.

Some stores have handmade versions of their own

Black Lives Matter signs, from coffee shops to auto shops, alongside rainbow flags and stickers on the windows that say ALL ARE WELCOME HERE. A lot don't, of course. The small dry cleaner that we pass has nothing but its hours written on the glass door, and a sign that says WE HAVE THE RIGHT TO REFUSE SERVICE. There's a skate shop with a few tall, bearded white men casually smoking outside it, and I don't expect to see a sign there either. But then another white man walks out the door, and the group calmly disperses to let him through. In the space between their bodies, I see a piece of cardboard wedged in the window, painted in dripping red: WE DON'T SERVE RACISTS.

It's all a far cry from what I'm used to seeing in Irvine. Mostly, there have been anti-masking signs and a few more Blue Lives Matter signs popping up, too, with the American flag boasting a single blue line through its typical red-and-white stripes. I've seen it around for years, a response when Black Lives Matter started when I was in elementary school or something—an assertion that the lives of police officers are important too. Honestly, it's weird that there are *more* signs since George Floyd was killed. I think maybe people don't realize that they're basically claiming that the lives of Black people and the lives of police officers are diametrically opposed. Or maybe they do know, and they just don't care.

Don't get me wrong, though: Irvine's pretty. Lots of green grass and trees, perfectly planned and planted, and the city has enough money to take meticulous care of the streets and sidewalks and every building down to the post office, so it always feels clean too. I like it. It's safe and predictable. That's what my parents love about it too. It's a wonder that Alexis is the one who chose to move away and Mel is the one who lives nearby—you'd think that they would have switched. Maybe I'll ask Mel about it when she wakes up. Which she will.

After a couple more blocks, Poirot brings me to the entrance of a small community park, with a playground and a baseball field whose metal gate is propped open. Within its tall fences are about a dozen people, with at least that many dogs. A dark-skinned South Asian man in a Lakers jersey is training his German shepherd puppy while the biggest ball of white fluff I've ever seen is rolling on its back in front of an elderly couple, who are laughing and chatting with each other in Korean. Behind them, a Shiba Inu is ignoring his owner, an Asian woman with straight black hair who looks like she's in her late twenties and who's trying to get him to sit for treats. A Black woman is shouting after two Chihuahuas who have stolen small bags of chips from a folding table someone has set up to apparently celebrate a birthday, and her friend—a white woman—is chasing after them.

Half the people here are wearing masks, though some of them only have it on haphazardly, with their noses fully exposed or the mask hanging around their chins. Since the protests, folks have been saying that it's actually totally safe—or at least safer—to be outside together, and it looks like people are taking advantage of that. Not to protest, of course, but to take their dogs outside and not feel guilty about it. I guess that works too.

Poirot starts to pull me toward the gate, and it's clear that Alexis must take him here often, because he's barking out little yips, tail up and swishing leisurely from one side to another. "You want to go in there, huh?" He yips again, and I decide that laughing *a little* isn't a total betrayal to my anti-pet sensibility. I mean, with his short snout, unwieldy tail, and comically large paws, he is objectively cute. I can admit that.

Once we're past the gate and closer to the middle of the field, I take his leash off, but that's when he hesitates. He looks up at me like he's asking for permission—or maybe just a sign that I'm not going to run off too. I wave in the direction of the other dogs. Poirot trots forward, slowly at first, and then breaks into a full-on scamper, playing chase with a bulldog that had given him a playful bow.

"Hey! Hey, close the door!" someone shouts. I turn to see that the gate is still ajar, and there's a person walking toward us with their own dog. They turn back as if to go and close it, but that's when someone else's dog takes off like a lightning bolt, racing toward the open gate as if their life depended on it.

No—not someone else's dog.

Alexis's dog.

CHAPTER FIVE

I RUN WITH A DEFICIENCY OF SPEED THAT would make my volleyball coach weep. It's not that I'm slow, but Poirot is *fast.* Who knew his short puppy legs could still make him sprint like a cheetah? But it's when he disappears through the open gate that I truly begin to worry: We had to cross a busy street to get here. What if he bolts into traffic? Suddenly, I'm running faster than I've ever thought possible, through the gate, around the fence that surrounds the baseball field, my mind racing with every fearful possibility–

Except that Poirot is perfectly fine. A girl about my age is now rubbing his belly as he wriggles around on the sidewalk, tongue lolling as usual.

"Oh my God," I breathe out. "Poirot." That's about all I can manage as I stop in front of them, my heart beating out of my chest. I bend and put my hands on my knees, my vision practically swimming as I thank all the gods that I don't have to tell my beloved older sister that I accidentally killed her dog.

"That's a cute name," the girl says. "Poirot? Like the detective?"

"Sure," I say. I guess that's common knowledge. Then, remembering that she is petting Poirot and not carrying his lifeless body from the street, I follow up with a thank-you. I gesture behind me. "Someone left the gate open. Someone who is, I swear, not me."

She giggles. "No problem. He came pretty easily when he saw the treats I had."

That's when I notice the German shepherd sitting dutifully behind her, like a bored but noble guard dog. I, of course, am lacking treats. I think that was one of the things Alexis mentioned: Always bring treats and doggie bags on a walk. I forgot both. Oops.

I step closer to the girl, and her guard dog turns his sharp amber eyes on me, his steady breathing suddenly paused. "Down," she says, and he relaxes immediately, lying by her side as if I suddenly disappeared.

"Wow. You're good at that."

"I'm a dog trainer," she says. "And it happens a lot. The baseball field is technically not supposed to be used as a dog park anyway. But, it's Covid right now."

She shrugs as she picks Poirot up for me to take. "Okay, bud, I think your mom is ready for you."

"Oh, I'm not—he's my sister's dog. She's at the store, so I took him out. I was trying to help, but I'm clearly not doing a very good job of it . . ." I trail off, hoping my self-deprecation is funny and not alarming.

"You'll get the hang of it," she says kindly as I return Poirot to his leash. She wipes her knees as she stands, and it's when she finally looks up at me that I stop breathing.

Wow, she's . . . wow. I wasn't really paying attention when I thought Poirot's life was on the line, but now I can see her friendly brown eyes that seem to smile through her round, wire-framed glasses. Her skin is a rich, deep brown and her hair is cropped close to the scalp, with a fashionable round line-part to the left. She's a couple inches shorter than me and wearing a mid-length skirt and a sweater vest over a button-down white shirt and tie.

"Do you go to private school?"

"What?" She looks at me in surprise and then blushes. "Oh. No. This is just how I dress."

"Oh." I nod like a fool. "You look nice."

"Thanks."

"I'm Tia," I offer, because it looks like she might be

getting ready to say something like, *Well, good luck with your dog. Bye.*

"Colby." She smiles. "And this is Gremlin, but I call him Grim," which is hilarious, because that is absolutely *not* what I would have guessed for a dog as refined as him. "I like your dog's name. Or, your sister's dog's name. She must love Agatha Christie."

Ahhhh, I know who that is! The old mystery lady writer person. "She does," I say, as if I know anything about what Alexis likes to read. Before now, I would've guessed she only read the newspaper and dusty books on modern art.

"I do too," she says. "It's always funny to think that she and Arthur Conan Doyle were contemporaries."

This conversation is going sideways. Soon, she's going to know I have no idea what she's talking about. "Are you, like, a full-time dog trainer or something?" I ask instead.

"I work part-time at Paw House," she says with a shrug. "I've done it for the last two years, so I decided to start their teen program for dog training too. I thought I'd get a chance to try something new when I went to college, but I guess the pandemic has other ideas."

"Are they planning for a remote first term or something?"

"Exactly."

"Ugh."

"I know."

She giggles again, which sounds a little bit like the wind chimes I pass by at the supermarket sometimes. I never realized what a pretty sound they made.

"Where are you going?" I ask, still not wanting the conversation to end.

"UC San Diego," she says with another shrug, like it's just a local school, and not a *really good* local school. "You?"

"Chapman University," I say. It's not a fancy UC, but it's close by, and Mel graduated from there, too, so I'm sure it'll get the job done. "Do you live near here?" I don't know what's sparking this sudden burst of boldness inside me, but I can't help it. It just feels like this girl is someone I should get to know.

"Yeah," she says. "Near that coffee shop on fifth." No idea what that means, but it sounds like it's close. "What about you?"

"My sister lives right around the corner. Like, ten minutes from here, tops."

"Cool," she says.

"Cool," I say.

"I should take Grim to the park now, though. He's been super patient."

"Oh," I say, and realize that I probably sound far too disappointed. "Oh!" I try again, this time with a cheerier tone. "Totally. Yeah. I think Poirot has had enough adventure for now." I actually think that's true. After spending the last couple minutes trying to chase a butterfly, he's now sleeping soundly on the pavement between us.

"Paw House is around the corner too," Colby adds as Grim lets out an impatient yawn. "You should bring Poirot sometime, if you want some tips. I work most days in the afternoon, if I'm not at the register."

I nearly jump out of my skin with a "Yeah, sure!" and she graces me with that wind chime laugh of hers again.

"Okay, cool. See you soon."

"You too," I say, and she calls Grim to his feet, walking around Poirot and me to the baseball field we just left. When she's out of sight, I bend toward Poirot and rub his baby belly. "Poirot," I whisper, thoughts still on Colby, "you terrible, wonderful little beast." He jumps up fast as if I've said magic words and barrels into my chest, licking my face and wagging his tail like he knew exactly what he was doing this entire time.

TEXT MESSAGE #2

MEL.

I met a girl. Like, not just a random girl, but like . . .

Like, wow.

She's stunning. And kind. And smart.

Alexis's stupid puppy brought me to her.

He ran away when I was taking him for a walk and then the girl (her name is Colby) she stopped him.

And then we talked, and we must talk again. It's like an absolute necessity.

So, I guess Poirot isn't stupid, after all.

Maybe he's cupid.

Like a dog cupid.

Anyway, so, so far North Hills isn't that bad. It's actually, like, really cool. I mean, it's kind of funky, and the street low-key smells, but I like the vibe. It's funny, because I would expect Alexis to still want to live someplace like Irvine, just given how she's so businesslike and efficient, and I'd expect you to live someplace like North Hills.

Not because you're messy! Lol

But because you're like . . . cool. I mean, Alexis is cool, too, but when I think about you, I think about you being so low-key, and down to earth, and also, it seems super gay here, which you also are, obviously.

Maybe the three of us can have a sister's weekend at Alexis's when you wake up.

I think we'd have a lot of fun.

So. Wake up soon. Okay?

CHAPTER SIX

ALEXIS GIVES ME A WEIRD LOOK THE NEXT morning when I ask if I can take Poirot for a walk. "It's gonna take a couple hours to get you back home if we leave too late," she reminds me. Right. I forgot that I was only staying for the weekend and it's already Sunday.

"About that," I say, thinking of the extremely cute girl I just met yesterday. "Finals are basically over, except for an essay for English I'm almost done with, and I can finish that tonight. Plus, it's been sort of nice . . . not being home with Mom and Dad. Is it okay if we play it by ear for the next day or so?" I try to give her my biggest puppy dog eyes, modeled, of course, after her fur beast.

She narrows her own eyes, and for a second I fear she might be on to me—even if the bit about Mom and

Dad is, technically, true. Then she bends down toward Poirot and tells him that his "auntie is falling for his good looks."

"I'm going to tell your dad the good news," she says to him, meaning she's going to tell Houston how much I love their dog. Ugh. I can't. But I also can't tell her that I'm using her dog to flirt with a girl I just met, so I'll let her think I've been body-swapped with someone who likes animals instead. Poirot's getting a walk either way, so I'm sure he doesn't care.

I double-check my teeth in the mirror and make sure that my gray T-shirt dress isn't stained with toothpaste or deodorant. Briefly, I consider not putting on a mask, because I think I look pretty cute today, and then I remember that I'm not in Irvine, and I don't want Colby to judge me. I pull up the address to Paw House on my phone as Poirot and I set off, taking a few quick turns around the neighborhood before we see the store nestled between a dry cleaner and a dim sum shop.

Poirot sniffs around a light pole while I take a couple calming breaths. Usually, if I think I like someone, I'm bound to see them at school or at least a place I know, like the mall or some fast-food place they're working at. But I haven't engaged with many humans offline in months, and definitely not someone *new*. It's both terrifying and kind of exciting. I almost want to stay in the in-between for longer, not knowing what's going to happen, but feeling excited for what's to come. But Poirot starts to lick the light pole like it's covered in candy, and I don't know if cement debris is toxic to dogs or something, so I pull him along and into the store.

Something is off the moment I walk in.

Though people are inside, it's eerily quiet, like everyone is trying to avoid being seen or heard. Poirot and I pass a long aisle of cat food, where a white woman peers around the corner, her hand hovering over a row of small tin cans. A white man on the other side of me is staring deeply into a salamander habitat, like he's hoping it will suck him in and away from wherever we are right now.

Poirot and I walk farther in, past a display of summer-themed chew toys for dogs, and I spot Colby at the register. She looks just as pretty as she did when I saw her yesterday, even in a black baseball cap and apron with *Paw House* emblazoned on the front. Putting on a smile, I move closer, until I realize that her face is streaked with tears.

"This is illegal," someone is saying–no, they're shouting–to her. "It's illegal, and it's disgusting, that in this country, we're expected to cover our faces like . . . like some third-world shithole. I want a manager—NOW."

"Ma'am," Colby says, her breath shaky. "The manager is going to say the same thing I'm saying, which is that—"

"I'm not wearing a fucking mask." The woman's tone is cold and forceful. She's at least twice our age: old enough to not scare a teenage girl. Before I can stop myself, I pick up Poirot, who is eagerly sniffing at a display of rawhide bones, and I position myself between the woman and Colby.

"Can I help you?" I say like *I'm* the manager, which, sure, I can cosplay today. I square my shoulders and give her the bossiest look I can muster.

The woman, who has dark blond curls and perfectly applied eyeliner, turns to sneer at me.

"You?" she spits.

"Actually, me." Another person intervenes, this time wearing an actual Paw House uniform. He's Asian, tall and muscular, with short black hair and thin, square glasses. "I'm Thomas, the manager, and you need to leave."

"Excuse me?" the woman says. "You think you can just bring the China virus here, and then tell me what to do? Are you aware I could sue you for harassment?"

"I'm filming you right now, lady," someone—another

white woman—says from an aisle behind us. She's standing in front of a wall of dog bowls. "I think we can make a pretty good case for who is harassing who."

The angry woman looks at the person filming her and then sucks in her cheeks. She squares her shoulders and puts her Gucci glasses on her face. "A patriot should be able to shop freely. You should all know your rights." She gives each of us our own personal glare and then turns and stalks out of the store.

Thomas turns to Colby, who's trying hard to stop her tears. "You can go on your break. Actually, you can take the day. We've got it from here."

"I'm sorry she said that to you," Colby whispers from behind her mask.

"Don't worry about it," he says, but his fists are balled. He nods toward me, like I'm her friend and not someone she just met yesterday. "Go ahead."

"Wait for me?" she asks, and when I nod, she turns and walks to the back of the store, removing her name tag as she goes.

A few minutes later, she emerges with smiling eyes, although I can tell they're still a little red. "Hi, Poirot," she says when she gets closer, and Poirot jumps into her arms gleefully, struggling to lick the parts of her face that aren't covered by the mask and wriggling his entire body against hers. For the second time in as many days,

I'm grateful to him. For his ability to make her smiling eyes crinkle a little more. Soon, I follow her out of the store, which feels natural, despite the scene we just left. With the hot air hitting our faces and the sound of life on the busy streets around us, it's almost like we're able to leave the entire memory behind.

Without talking about it, we let Poirot take the lead, following where he sniffs down the sidewalk. We don't speak, but it doesn't feel awkward. Colby seems lost in her own thoughts anyway. Her eyes are downcast and she's walking slowly. I try to match her pace as much as Poirot will let me.

After we pass a few more stores, Colby pauses in step and finally speaks. "This is gonna sound so ironic, but—do you mind if I take off my mask?"

"Go for it," I say, and she does. I take mine off too. The heat was making walking with the mask feel more tedious than usual.

"Is there anywhere in particular you want to go?" she asks.

"Oh, I . . . literally had no plans today other than to take Poirot to the pet store." Which, now that I say it out loud, might sound either sad, or creepy, or both.

"That's sweet," she says. "You're sweet. You didn't have to . . . thank you for standing up for me."

"It's really not a big deal," I say. It's something Alexis would probably do, to be honest. I wonder if she'd be proud of me. "Are you okay?"

"Sure." Her laugh is hollow. "I mean, that happens like twice a week these days. Sometimes more. It's one of the worst ones so far, but not unusual."

"Are you serious?"

She nods like it's nothing, but it makes me want to hug her close to me. No one should get treated like that, and certainly not on a regular basis.

"Thomas and some of the other staff get it worse, though. I mean, he's Vietnamese, first of all, lady, and second, just . . . fuck off!" She kicks at a rock underneath her, and it rolls to the side, instead of in front of her.

"Yeah, fuck off!" I say, and kick the rock, too, hoping it'll make her smile.

It does.

"That was a good kick," she says as the rock skitters off the sidewalk, across the street, and into a distant bush.

"My volleyball skills at work," I say, which doesn't make sense, and she knows it, but instead of questioning me, she scrunches up her nose and gives almost a snort-giggle, which is, as it turns out, my new-new favorite sound ever. My God, this can't be how people fall in love, right? *Right?*

Be still my teenage heart.

We keep walking, and Colby stays quiet, but I don't mind. Even with her lips pursed and her brow furrowed, there's a radiance to her, a life to that determined expression that pulls me toward her, because beneath her sadness is a fire, stubborn and bold. There must be, because she just had someone screaming at her in public, and she managed to stand her ground—is still standing now. She was crying, sure, but who wouldn't be? Teenagers like us just trying to do our shitty part-time jobs? I've only had one part-time job before—a summer internship, last year—and if I had to go back, every day, in the middle of a pandemic, knowing I might get screamed at by complete strangers multiple times a week . . . well, I don't know if *I* could handle it.

The thought occurs to me that I don't even think I'd be *allowed* to work under those conditions. "Your parents don't mind that you're working a job in person?" I ask.

She blinks up at me, the sudden query breaking the renewed silence. "What? Oh." She stops walking, and I tug gently on Poirot's leash, which suits him just fine, because there are several clumps of grass in front of the apartment complex beside us that apparently need his thorough investigation. Colby sighs deeply. "Well, about that." She laughs. "We had a big fight actually. I stopped working in March and then started again at the end of April, because I needed to get out of the house. Both of my parents refused, because of um . . ." She pauses. "Some family stuff that happened earlier in the year. Because of the pandemic. But I guess they saw that I was struggling, being out of school, too, and Paw House *does* have a strong mask policy . . . which, you know, my parents love–and other people, obviously, absolutely detest."

Yup. I did indeed just witness that. I nod in response just as Poirot begins to arch his body on the grass. I awkwardly excuse myself to clean up after him. Thankfully, there's a public trash can right beside us; I know Colby works at a pet store, but I can't imagine walking next to such a beautiful girl while holding dog waste in a bag. Gross.

"You said Poirot is your sister's dog, right?" Colby asks once we begin walking again. We round a corner onto a shaded neighborhood street.

"Yeah."

"So, do you live with her, or someplace nearby?"

"I live in Irvine," I say. "With my parents. I'm just visiting."

"Oh," she says. She looks disappointed, and that kind of makes me happy, which then makes me wonder if I'm a bad person. "How long are you here?" she asks.

"For, uh . . ." I clear my throat. "A few more days." Alexis technically hasn't agreed to that, but I'm sure it's fine.

Colby turns to me, beaming with a smile that could rival the sun. "That's great," she says, and I grin back, until Poirot leaps forward to bark angrily at a pigeon poking at a piece of pizza. "It's fine, buddy; the pigeon didn't do anything to you." I tug him toward me, but I must pull too hard, because he skitters onto his back. "Oh! Damn, I'm sorry!" I scoop him up, feeling like both an awful aunt and also a terrible romantic prospect. But Colby is still smiling.

"He's very cute," she says. She comes closer and gently rubs his belly again. He squirms happily. I put him back down, and he starts sniffing normally, as if he hadn't just been splayed out on the sidewalk two seconds ago.

"At least you're resilient," I mutter.

"Puppies usually are," Colby says. She cocks her head at me. "Do you have a lot of experience with dogs?"

"No," I answer truthfully, and then panic. "I mean, we've never had a dog before, but Alexis adopted one, like probably everyone else in the pandemic, and her husband has to travel to LA for work, so I'm, you know, helping with the dog. Poirot."

Colby raises an eyebrow. "So, did you come into Paw House to shop for him, or . . ."

I blow out my cheeks, feeling caught. "Well. I mean. Also, you mentioned that you worked there, so . . ." She giggles softly, and when I look at her, it looks like she's genuinely charmed. Thank God.

"I'm glad you came," she says. "My hero."

Oh, my cheeks hurt too much. I don't think I've smiled this wide in my life. I try hard to school my facial expression into something more nonchalant, and that's when I notice how hard Poirot is panting. He's staring at us both, ears relaxed, eyes semi-closed, tongue lolling, and breathing so intensely I'm suddenly afraid his lungs will give out.

"I should take him home," I say.

"Of course," Colby responds, bending to give Poirot a quick rub behind the ears. I take out my phone to look up the directions back to Alexis's house, since I actually don't know where we are now. I hope Colby will say something else—like maybe ask to hang out again. But she just stands and waits patiently as I stare too hard at my phone. I could take it as a loss—shrug it off and move on, call this a nice walk, with a nice girl, and then head on home. Or . . . I could try a new approach.

Something different.

"Um," I pause. Earlier, it felt like I was channeling Alexis, standing there between that angry woman and Colby. Now I try to channel Mel and that effortless swag she's always seemed—*seems*—to have. I imagine wiping my hand on my shirt, because I'm sure it's sweaty from the nerves, but I can't actually do that, because that's a little too honest. Instead, I lift my phone up like a good luck charm. "Want me to walk you home first?"

And then Colby smiles. Again. Beautiful, megawatt, rival to the sun. Big brown eyes, and a little gap between her two front teeth, and absolutely nothing, *nothing*, has felt like this before. No, not even looking at the poster of Amber Liu that hangs on my bedroom wall.

This is, like, one hundred times better.

Colby gently reaches for my still-raised hand and pulls my phone toward her so she can see the screen. She moves her finger over it, and the map shifts. "I live here," she says. "Not too far from you." When she looks up at me, I realize she's so close that I can see the gentle curl of her eyelashes. My breath catches.

"Okay," I say, and I don't know if that counts as us coming to some sort of agreement, but it must, because soon we're walking again, except now Colby is leading us. She takes my hand—the one that's not holding Poirot's leash—and I pretend that I'm not going to go into cardiac arrest. Within minutes, she stops us at the large, see-through doors of a massive, modern apartment building that towers above us. We must not have walked very far from Paw House at all. Probably, we were going in very slow circles.

"So," we both say at the same time, and then she giggles, and dammit, I giggle too. A beat passes, and then she stands on her tiptoes and wraps her arms around my neck. She's so close, and fits so perfectly in my arms, that I wonder how it's the first time, and not the fiftieth. When she pulls away, the loss is stronger than I could have imagined.

"Thank you," she says again.

"Totally," I say, which is incredibly suave and debonair, if I do say so myself.

"What are you doing in an hour?"

"Uh . . . homework? Well, an essay. For finals."

"Boo, finals," she says. "We finished this week. But okay," she says. "Can I have your phone?" I hand it to her automatically, unlocking it as requested, and try to hide my excitement when I realize she's putting in her number. "Call me when you're done," she says.

When she returns my phone, our fingers touch.

There's a breath of hesitation, and for the briefest moment, I wonder if she'd let me kiss her. If she'd want me to. It would be the first time I've kissed a girl, and the second time I've kissed anyone, and I know I've only just met her, but maybe . . .

"Oh!" She jumps back, and I look down to see Poirot licking her leg. "I'll see you soon." She laughs, bending over to rub his head quickly. She stands and presses a few buttons into the keypad beside her door, and when it buzzes, she disappears inside—but not before turning around and giving me a quick, fleeting kiss on my cheek.

Poirot trots ahead, but I float the rest of the way home.

TEXT MESSAGE #3

Mel. I can't. My heart is flying out of my chest.

She gave me her number. SHE GAVE ME HER NUMBER. SHE

. . . this is a flirt, right? Not a "let's be friends" thing but a "we're both gay" thing, right?

RiGhT?

What if she doesn't actually want me to call? What if she was being nice?

I'll text her first. Just so she has my number.

Okay. Sent.

BuT wHaT iF sHe HaTeS mE

. . . oh. She texted back.

She DOES want to hang out again tonight

YAY

WAIT

NO

GAH

CHAPTER SEVEN

"TIA, YOU MET HER YESTERDAY," ALEXIS reminds me as she switches on the next episode of *Tiger King*. It's a docuseries about a weird guy who runs a questionable zoo and the equally questionable animal conservationist who hates him. It premiered on Netflix a couple months ago, and we're both finally watching it for the first time. It's fascinating, but right now, I can't focus on anything that's not the adorable gap between Colby's two front teeth and her pretty brown eyes.

"I know," I say, lying on my back while I stare at Alexis's living room ceiling. I am not actually doing my English essay, because the gay panic has set in and I don't know how to exist anymore. "*I know*." I'm saying it like I'm fake crying, because I know it's ridiculous to feel this strongly about someone you just met, but she . . . and I . . . and like . . . it just . . . "I just really like her."

"What about Drew?"

"What about him?" That's probably not the right answer. "I mean." Now I sit up, my love bubble burst into tiny, painful flames. "I told you: I don't like him that way."

"I know," Alexis says. "But does he know that? Have you talked to him yet? I think that's the best course of action. And do you want Ethiopian or Indian?" She lifts up her phone to demonstrate that she's ordering food.

"Ethiopian. And I talk to him every day."

"*About this*, Tia. Talking to him *about this* is probably the best course of action."

Gross. I hate when she gives reasonable advice. I go back to staring at the ceiling, but this time my expression is sour, as if it just cursed me out. "*I don't wanna*," I mutter. I look over at my sister with a pout. She's looking down at her phone, but now she's frowning. I wonder if she's gotten another update about Mel, which is annoying, because no one is texting *me* with updates about Mel, and last I checked, I'm her sister too.

"Houston's boss is being a butt," she says, explaining the text she was reading. That makes me feel a little better—although, you know, sad for Houston.

"Apparently their Covid precautions are abysmal. He's trying to cut his trip short."

"Does that mean I can't stay longer?" I ask. My voice has an unmistakable whine.

Alexis waves her hand. "Stay as long as you want. I texted Mom and Dad about it when you asked this morning, so they're fine with it. Although"—she gives me a pointed look—"I'm pretty sure you didn't pack for more than a few days."

"We'll cross that bridge when we get to it," I squeal. I wrap her in an enthusiastic hug that she shrugs out of so she can keep texting her husband. Rude. Instead, I give my pent-up affection to Poirot, who is snoring soundly on Alexis's lap, until the screen on my own phone lights up. I grab it, hoping it's an update about Mel, or at least a cute text from Colby. She hasn't responded since my potentially overenthusiastic yes! to hanging out. Maybe I shouldn't have added the exclamation point.

Unfortunately, Drew's name pops up instead, followed by his text: So, am I ever gonna see you again? My hands drop as I fall backward onto the couch. This day was going so well. I *could* tell him that I'm officially staying in San Diego longer, return date TBD, because I met a cute girl and I don't want to leave, but I don't think that would go over well. Instead, I type, delete, and retype several different messages, before landing on: Of course you are! I decide to snap him a pic of myself smiling with my eyes closed and tongue out for good measure. He responds with a similar one of him, too, and that's what we spend the next hour doing, communicating primarily through increasingly silly selfies. I don't know if that counts as "talking," but I guess sometimes, doing *something* is better than doing nothing at all.

Soon our texting finds a natural lull so I start panic-reading my short text exchange with Colby instead. The Ethiopian food arrives soon after. Alexis spreads out the two plates of injera and a vegan platter on the coffee table just as Colby finally responds.

How about the park tonight? Bring Poirot, if your sister's okay with it.

I sit up straight, my fingers jabbing at the screen.

She's fine with it! What time?

She suggests six P.M. and I turn desperately to Alexis, who is simultaneously texting and petting the sleeping Poirot. "Alexis, can I steal Poirot tonight? For the park, around the corner? Colby wants to meet up."

Alexis rolls her eyes, but she's smiling. "Fine," she

says. "Only because it won't be that dark out, and he still needs to go out before bed. But text me when you arrive and when you leave, okay?"

"Okay, Mom."

She sticks her tongue out at me in a decidedly unparental fashion, and I stick mine out too. Then, just as I send back a simple **sure** to Colby—no exclamation point—a video call from Drew comes through. I don't want to admit that I'm annoyed, so I plaster on a fake smile as I answer. But his usually bright brown face is dull and slack. The white around his brown eyes is tinged with red, and the skin is dark and puffy. It takes me a second, but I realize he's been crying.

"Robbie was just arrested," he says through shuddery breaths.

"What?" I sit up straight, a stone suddenly in my throat.

He takes a shaky inhale. "Robbie. The protest was today—I—didn't you see the link I sent you?"

I did, yesterday. I didn't look at it closely, but I don't tell him that. And I didn't realize Robbie had gone too; he's not even in our social studies class. Maybe something else went down in a different period too. Or a different class entirely. Maybe a lot of things have gone down at school, and Drew knows all about it, and all our friends know all about it, and I'm just . . . here. But now at least I realize why he stopped texting. He must've been at the protest.

He's still talking. "I guess it got out of hand. Counterprotesters showed up, which is wild. Like, what are you countering? Turns out it was a bunch of parents from the school, and they tried to complain that we were gathering in a group when there's supposed to be those quarantine measures, but that's crap. I know for a fact that, like, half of them have been at anti-masking protests. And then Robbie got mad and threw a balled-up piece of paper—the police said it was a glass bottle—but, like, from where? We weren't drinking. And I *saw* the paper. And then, I don't know, they grabbed him, and he's in jail now." He wipes his eyes. "I can't believe I'm crying."

"You're allowed to cry." I'm still in shock, but crying seems entirely reasonable.

"I shouldn't be surprised," Drew says. "But, man, first this dude is killed, and now our classmates are being arrested for being at a protest *about* him getting killed. This country is so fucked up," he says. "Like, you hear about it, and then you *see* it, and like . . ." He takes another shaky breath. "Every time I get in the car to go somewhere on my own, I see this fear in my mom's eyes, and I want to be like, chill, man. It's a two-minute drive to the store. But then, I remember, because I look like this guy—George Floyd, this guy who looks like me, like *us*—I remember that it's more than a possibility that I won't come back."

The idea of Drew not coming back makes me want to vomit. I clutch the phone tighter in my hand. "I'm sorry," I say, because there's nothing else to say.

"You shouldn't be sorry," he says. "It's not like you're the cop who killed him, or terrorized every other Black person in the country."

If this call is going to turn into a rundown on how the average Black American life expectancy is significantly shorter than literally everyone else's, I'm going to lose my mind. I change the subject, because I have to. "Do you know how to get in touch with Robbie?"

"I've been talking to his mom," he says. "I mean, you know. She's calm. Said it was bound to happen sooner or later. Surprised he's never been arrested before." He rolls his eyes. "Which is *insane.* Robbie's a straight A student. He's never been in trouble. Why should she have to expect him to be arrested?"

"I'm sorry," I say again. I know how he feels. I mean, I understand that he's feeling upset, and angry, for our friend, a boy we both know and care for. I recognize that he must be feeling scared and anxious. But I don't feel anything. In fact, I feel completely numb.

"We're getting bail together now, so he should be out by the morning," Drew continues, "but I'm so mad. We're planning another protest tomorrow. At the police station." I know the one. Dad took me once when I was twelve, after he'd been pulled over yet again for a broken taillight that was not, in fact, broken. It's the common excuse a Black man hears before a gun is pulled on him. At least, that's what my dad says. *This is my daughter*, he'd said to the officer who greeted him when we walked in. *She's a child. A person. I just wanted you to see her and recognize that fact the next time you pull me over.*

"Is that safe?" I ask Drew automatically. I mean, Robbie was just arrested for protesting. It doesn't seem like the smartest decision to try to join him.

"Does it matter? This country wants us dead anyway."

The words slap me in the face. I hate that he said that. It's an awful, cruel thing to say, and suddenly I feel like I'm existing on two different planes. One where one of my big sisters is merely sleeping in, late and luxurious, and on a visit to the other, I've met a beautiful girl, whom I've never had to see cry. Maybe we're in the park where we met. Maybe there are people—Black, white, South Asian, Korean—sitting at picnic tables, and on blankets, and no one is masked, because we're all healthy. Their dogs are yapping at the birds in the trees, and the squirrels are darting across the grass to find a morsel of food. Toddlers with long lives ahead of them are escaping from the playground while their parents chase after them, calling their names playfully, like there's nothing to worry about past the asphalt. Like them, I feel perfectly safe here. Fully alive.

The other plane is where Drew's words exist. Angry, coarse, and full of bitterness.

"Drew," I say. He's telling me the details of the protest he's planning next, but I can't hear them right now. "Drew, I gotta go."

I don't wait to hear him say goodbye.

INTERLUDE #2

THE FIRST TIME I SAW ALEXIS BREAK, I WAS ten years old. She was twenty-five.

I was sitting with Mom and Dad on our couch, watching a *Bridezillas* rerun. Mel was on a date with a girl who wasn't going to last the week, which we all knew, because she already had a crush on a different girl she'd met at a concert two days before. We'd even placed bets, because it was funny, even though Mel said we were jerks, and that we were taking nonchalant allyship too far. Alexis was in the kitchen, shoulders tense, brow furrowed as she looked at her laptop. She was keeping track of the news. Then—

"It's coming. They're about to announce the verdict."

Suddenly, the mood in the room changed. My

parents sat up straighter. Dad leaned forward and changed the channel to the local news station. Mom put her hands on the pearls around her neck. Alexis came and sat next to me, her arm around my shoulder, like she was trying to protect me, though I didn't understand why.

"Do you think they'll convict him?" Alexis asked.

Dad took a deep breath and raised his shoulders. Mom just pursed her lips.

"It's pretty cut-and-dried to me, though." Alexis kept talking. "Trayvon did absolutely nothing wrong. He went to the store, and Zimmerman, who isn't even a police officer, thought he looked suspicious and shot him. That's murder, right? Plain and simple. You can't just kill someone because you don't like their vibe."

Still, our parents didn't respond. I looked at them and then at Alexis. They were talking about a Black kid who'd been shot the year before. I heard about him, knew what he looked like. Based on what Alexis was saying, it seemed to make sense. A kid was killed. Why wouldn't the adult who killed him go to prison?

"It's such an *obvious* win," Alexis went on, like she was trying to convince us that there wasn't any other option. Like there was no point in us even watching, because of course, Trayvon would get justice.

Of course, the killer would go to jail. Of course, of course, of course.

But that's not what happened.

The killer was acquitted—of all charges. He got to walk away scot-free, and I got to watch my big sister sob as my mom put her arms around her, whispering like it could be some comfort to hear, "It's okay, baby. This happens. It happens all the time."

CHAPTER EIGHT

I LEAVE THE HOUSE JUST BEFORE SIX. POIROT trots happily alongside me, ears bobbing with each step as faded pinks and reds bleed into the sky. I could be annoyed that he's coming with me on this potential date, but I'm not. I like seeing his tail high and proper, like a periscope curled into a question mark. He's not aware of protests or pandemics, bullets or hospital beds. He's only thinking about the sniffs in the air, the feel of concrete beneath his paws, this moment here—and the fact that, probably, we're on our way to his favorite place on earth: some patches of grass in the soft brown earth, filled with the potential for play. It's simple, and beautiful, and I shouldn't be jealous of a dog, but now my eyes are tearing up, and I feel like screaming for the rest of eternity.

But there's Colby. She's waiting alongside Grim. Alone among the grass patches in the empty baseball field, she's a beacon in the onset of evening and looking decidedly more radiant now than when I saw her last. Like she hadn't been crying just hours ago. Like Drew had been barely an hour ago.

But Colby—now. Right now. She's out of her Paw House uniform, wearing a yellow sundress with clean white sneakers and a white paper mask. She tightly grips a brown leather leash that Grim wears proudly, like a fashion statement rather than a legal requirement. I wonder, for a moment, if maybe Colby likes fashion, if she's the type of girl to put together Pinterest boards, and flip through magazines, and watch beauty videos, because she strikes me as thoughtful, prepared. I don't know a lot of girls our age with close-cropped haircuts that they rock with such boldness, and it suits her. She must know it does. The way her eyes crinkle with a smile beneath the mask, the way she stands: It's like she knows who she is. And I like that.

At first, Poirot pauses, tail wagging uncertainly, and then he must recognize both Colby and Grim, because suddenly he's pulling with all the force his little body can muster, yipping with unbridled excitement. If he wasn't so incredibly small, it'd be a lot harder to hold him back. "Heeey," I say as I struggle to follow him forward. "Calm down, calm down." Finally, I bend down to pick him up. "Chill out, P."

When I look up again, Colby is looking at me with a light in her eyes that makes my mouth go dry. But when she catches me staring back, she clears her throat and drops her gaze and takes a few steps away, although we weren't standing very close.

"Okay, so, hi," she says.

I move my own mask down to my chin and aim for a smile to ease her nerves. "Hey," I say.

She gestures to the expanse of the field. "So, I thought maybe I could teach you a few tips and tricks for Poirot, since he's still a little . . ."

"Bandit? Escape master? Two-foot terror?"

She giggles. Mission accomplished.

"Yeah, that," she says. "Are you up for it?" I am, but I'm a little surprised. Is that why she called me out here at night? To train my dog? She must hear my thoughts, because her shoulders slump a little. "Or not. I'm sorry. I just thought—I wanted to make up for this afternoon."

"Make up for what? You didn't do anything wrong."

"Okay, maybe not make up for anything, but like . . . to thank you. For, you know, being so sweet to me. But, I guess this is sort of a dumb idea."

"Are you kidding?!" Immediately, I hold up Poirot like Rafiki holding Simba in *The Lion King*. "I could use all the help I can get with this thing. Er, this . . . beast. Creature. I swear I'm not a horrible human. But I would LOVE your help. Your astute and supreme expertise. Please. I insist. No, in fact—I beg."

The corners of her eyes crinkle. "Really?"

"Truly. I am your humble student."

"Okay, then." She straightens her shoulders again and then pulls her mask down around her chin. "Put Poirot down."

That's the first step. The next is to let him sniff the grass and then, once he's feeling calm, get him to sit. Then lie down. Then sit up again. This is what's called a "puppy push-up," and I know Poirot already knows how to do this because Alexis showed off his skills to me earlier in the day. Even though I didn't ask. Poirot only knows a few of the commands, thus far, but even these seem to delight Colby, who claps her hands together with enthusiasm.

"Great!" she says. "Okay, so he's got some basic obedience."

I look down at Poirot, feeling proud, like he's my weird son or something. "Good job, bud."

Then Colby turns to Grim, who's lying on the ground, eyes closed, probably bored out of his skull. When he notices Colby's attention on him, though, he opens his golden eyes, eyebrows raised expectantly. "Sit," she says, and he climbs slowly to his feet, stretching his back languidly and then coming to a regal, seated pose.

"Look," she says, and he keeps his eyes on her, which I'm sure is easy to do. Even to another creature, she must be something to behold.

"Stay," she says, and puts one hand up. Then she backs up, first one step, then three, then ten. It's only at this last point that Grim's ears perk up, like a few feet is fine, but he's not ready to be abandoned.

Colby turns back to me. "Okay, ready to try that with Poirot?"

It . . . goes about as well as can be expected with a two-month-old puppy. Poirot follows me almost every time, except for the moments he follows a leaf, or a lightning bug, or the flop of Grim's tail. The third time he goes for Grim's tail, Grim slowly pushes his nose against Poirot's head, takes a deep sniff, and then licks his head.

My own laughter surprises me. Grim is *huge* and could probably eat Poirot with one chomp if he chose to, but instead, he's treating Poirot like nothing more than an annoying little brother. And then suddenly I miss Mel until my stomach aches.

God, Mel.

Even though I sort of grew up as an only child, since Mel and Alexis were both in middle school and high school by the time I was born, they were always around, wreaking havoc, doing their duty making me feel like the annoying-but-protected little sister. And now I might go from having two overprotective sisters to just one, and if Alexis really isn't doing as well as she's trying to show she is, then I may not be left with either.

"You okay?"

I blink and realize Colby's gotten close to me. I can see how deep the dimple on her left cheek is and the gentle curve of her lips, frowning now that she thinks she's lost me in a world of my own, far from hers. I don't want to be far from her. In fact, if I took just one breath closer, our lips would be touching, and maybe she wouldn't be frowning anymore. If only I dared to take that breath . . .

"I'm fine," I breathe instead. "Sorry. Just . . . do you have siblings?"

She cocks her head at me. "Yes," she says. "My older brother just graduated college."

"Mine too," I almost shout, like it's some sort of miracle that we share the incredibly common experience of having older siblings. But, I like that we have something else in common—more threads that have the power to tie us together. "Er, well, I have a sister. Another sister, I mean. One, obviously, is Poirot's mom,

Alexis. The other sister, Mel, graduated from grad school most recently, like two years ago."

She smiles and the earth warms. "Right. We're both little sisters."

"Tragic," I say.

And I take in her smile, and the heat that spreads across my cheeks, even as she steps away, and talks to Grim, and tells me more about how to train Poirot. And even though it's dark, and my world seems to be in a constant flux of uncertainty, being here with her, and Grim, and Poirot makes me feel, for the first time in a long time, the tiniest bit steady.

As we spend the evening together, the things I learn about Colby are thus: She started training Grim a year ago, when her dad bought his skinny, two-month-old body from a shady dog dealer on Craigslist. He'd been looking for a deal on a motorcycle, when persistent pop-ups of cheap German shepherds kept crowding the page. He finally clicked on one, saw Grim in a sad and sorry state, brought him home, and lo, Colby tells me—her first love.

That's why she decided she might as well get certified, even though she doesn't want to be a dog trainer.

Instead, she wants to learn how to kayak, and how to sail, and maybe, one day, buy a small boat to live on, at least for a little while. As far as jobs, she's low on inspiration, she tells me, but as far as life, that sounds ideal.

I tell her my dad composes music; my mom is a translator and loves to sing. I tell her Alexis is a project manager at some corporate firm; that Mel graduated with a degree in psychology. I tell her this is ironic. I don't tell her why.

And what do I want to do? What do I want to be?

In this moment, honestly?

Alive.

CHAPTER NINE

DREW DOESN'T RESPOND WHEN I TEXT HIM IN the morning, even though I'm trying to be a good friend and ask about Robbie. I want to text Robbie, too, but I don't know what I would say. *Sorry you're in jail; hope everything works out?* That doesn't seem helpful. So, I let the pit in my stomach fester while I try to focus instead on the flirtatious texts Colby and I are sending each other. They're interspersed with pictures of us with our dogs—because yes, I need her to continue to think I'm a dog person.

And I mean, listen, I will admit that Poirot's grown on me these last couple days. His tail has started to wag when he sees me, and if I'm on the couch, he'll try to lie on my legs and stomach. It's not the worst feeling in the world. He's like a small, weighted blanket. Heavy and solid, in a comforting sort of way. Plus, earlier today, he plopped next to my leg when I proofread and sent in my English essay: the very last assignment of my high school career.

So, it's not a *total* lie when I send Colby another pic of him with his eyes bugging out and his tongue lolling with a text that says **Wild but worth it.**

Like me, she types back, and I try not to split my face open with a grin. **Some friends from work are having a party tonight. Want to come?**

My immediate thought is *Yes, of course*. In what universe would I say no?

But when I tell Alexis, she stares at me with huge, concerned eyes. "Are you serious?"

We're standing in the kitchen as she rinses the dishes, and I help put them in the dishwasher. Her question makes me pause, though, and I stand up straight, looking at her head-on. "Yes?"

"Tia," Alexis says. She turns the faucet off and dries her hands before facing me. "There's a pandemic. We're supposed to be staying inside. Away from people."

I roll my eyes. "Okay, sure. But I've already hung out with Colby, and you didn't have a problem with it."

"One, I didn't know you were going to hang out

with her the first time, and the second time, it was just the two of you, in an open space."

"You went to the grocery store the other day."

"Because I had to! Do you know how hard it's been to order groceries online? All the websites are backed up. You going to a party full of random people you don't know isn't a necessity."

I know that what she's saying makes sense, but also, this is probably one of the first parties I've ever been invited to. When March and everything that it brought came around this year, I figured any chances I may still have had were gone forever. And plus, it's Colby. I trust her. I bet everyone will be masked up and sitting six feet away from each other or whatever. Probably.

Still, Alexis thinks this is the end of the conversation and switches topics, asking me what I thought of last night's *Tiger King* episode that neither of us was paying attention to. I don't push it, because I don't want to argue, but also, Alexis is my sister, not my mom. She can give me her opinion, but she can't tell me what to do. I never do anything I'm not supposed to. I'm a good kid, I listen to my parents, I follow the rules, I get decent enough grades, and I've made out with one person in my life. Plus, today is technically my last real day of high school and my other sister is in the hospital while my best friend refuses to talk to me. I deserve to be a little celebratory. What's the worst that could happen?

I don't tell Colby I need a ride. I don't want to make her complicit. Instead, I wait until Alexis goes to sleep, and then I walk to the nearest bus stop, hoping I won't get killed. After a few minutes, it strikes me that I'm standing here at eleven o'clock at night, alone, and without having told anyone where I am. This is maybe not the smartest plan I've ever hatched. But the bus shows up a few minutes later, and I'm grateful to see that not only are my fellow passengers masked, like me, but there are plenty of seats, so it's not crowded out at all, meaning low risk of disease transmission, and there's no one I can see that makes my hair stand on end.

See, Alexis? Perfectly safe! Probably!

When I get off at my stop, I text Colby that I'm nearly there.

Great, she responds. **Look for the pig.**

I blink at my phone. *Look for the* . . . I look around at the cute rows of quirky-colored homes and the various rainbow flags and IN THIS HOME, WE BELIEVE IN SCIENCE signs perched in front of people's windows. It's a funky, youthful neighborhood, but nothing indicates that a farm is nearby. Is it a . . . metaphorical pig? A poster of a pig? What am I looking for, exactly?

I decide to stick to the directions on my phone and wander down a long, tree-lined street, until I see the words *you have arrived* pop up on the screen. Unfortunately, not one of these houses has a clear view of their house numbers, and far too many of them are marked with 1/2s and 1/4s, like each home has been split into different apartment units.

I keep walking, peering creepily through people's fenced-in front yards, until I see it: a huge, spotted pot-bellied pig laid out beneath the low branches of a tree, beside the porch of what Alexis would call a "classic craftsman." Behind the pig is a wooden doghouse—er, pig house—with a metal nameplate that says BAM-BAM.

Okay then.

I walk closer to the porch and hear music coming through the screen door. When I open the gate, I'm careful to close it behind me lest Bam-Bam discover lightning-fast reflexes like Poirot on our first visit to the park. But she does little more than grunt in my direction, her eyes fluttering open and then closed as I walk past her. "Hello?" I call through the screen.

"Back here!" someone answers.

I open the door and follow the music, which becomes louder as I meander through a small white kitchen and a quaint but very cramped living room, on the other side of which is another screen door leading to the backyard. Outside, about a dozen other teenagers are hanging out, some of them sitting in a small inflatable pool filled with shallow water, and others gathered around a foldable white table, several red solo cups arranged carefully on opposing sides. As I expected, everyone is masked, including me. Only those who are drinking have their masks pulled down, around their chins.

"Tia!" I hear my name before I see Colby, but it doesn't bother me one bit when she wraps her arms around my neck, launching herself at me like we haven't seen each other in ages. "Guys, this is my friend Tia!"

Colby's coworkers nod in my general direction and mutter various greetings, but those at the table are focused on their game.

"So, where are we?" I ask, wondering how a bunch of teenagers managed to commandeer an entire house during the pandemic.

Colby points to an Asian guy and two Black guys seated around a squat, shoddy wicker table next to the pool. "That's Brian, Marcus, and Jackson. They're roommates and freshmen at San Diego State. This is their house. Or, the one their parents are renting for them, I guess."

The three boys wave at me pleasantly before returning to what looks to be a very intense game of Spades.

"And . . . they have a pig," I confirm, as if Bam-Bam was a nighttime illusion.

"I'm gonna be a vet!" Marcus responds enthusiastically. That doesn't really answer the question, but everyone smiles and moves on, so I do too. A *whoop* sounds behind us, and I turn to look back at the table, where someone in a Padres jersey is doing a victory dance that looks like the Running Man.

"They look happy," I say with amusement.

"Do you want to play?" Colby asks.

"Um . . ." I blush. On a scale of *absolutely* to *painfully*, how uncool does it make me that I have no idea what they're playing? "Uh . . ."

"It's beer pong," Colby says. She smiles at me like I'm the most adorable thing in the world. That helps. "Basically, each team tries to get the little ball into one of the cups, and each time you do, the opposing team has to drink. It's pretty much an excuse to get very drunk."

"Ah." This is nothing like watching reruns of *The Judy Garland Show* in my living room with Drew while eating Skittles and Sour Punch. But that's why I snuck out of the house, right? Here was an opportunity to do something different, to be a different kind of me. And to interact with people my age again. "Sure," I say.

After the last red cup has been conquered by the previous teams, the winners reset the table. Now it's my and Colby's turn. We get paired against Honor, who's white, and Sumi, who's Asian, and I'm pretty sure the two of them consider beer pong an Olympic-level sport. They look at us with narrowed eyes and fierce determination, Honor leaning forward like she can't wait to smash the ball in our faces.

"They're actually really fun," Colby whispers to me as she pulls her mask to her chin. I enjoy the feel of her breath against my cheek as she leans close to me like we're in on a secret just for the two of us. "But they're competitive. They go to a different school than I do, but I've gone to a couple of their soccer games. It is terrifying."

"Are you two ready, or are you already planning to forfeit?" Sumi asks. I take another look at her–when the hell did she put on a sweatband? Maybe she was wearing it before, and I didn't notice. Either way, her neck-length black hair is pulled out of her eyes, and she's throwing the white Ping-Pong ball up and down in one hand, tapping her foot impatiently. I'm tempted to back out, but Colby looks so game–she's bouncing up and down, ready to go. It is *so* cute.

I can do this. I take my spot next to Colby and crack my neck, getting into the spirit of the game. This is going to be fun. I lace my fingers together and push them out and then shake out my shoulders. "Let's do this!"

Honor takes the first shot, and the ball lands in the red cup closest to her on our side. "Ha!" She and Sumi bump chests. Colby sighs dramatically and takes the cup, downing the beer in two sips. I'm thankful that she's gone first—I'm not prepared to admit that I've never had beer before either.

She puts the cup to the side and then hands me the ball. "Ready?"

I put on my most carefree expression. "Totally." Thanks to my three years of volleyball, I feel fairly confident in my hand-eye coordination. Sure, I'm used to hitting a much bigger ball over a giant net, not popping a tiny white ball into a small red cup, but I figure it's roughly the same. It's more similar than *soccer* anyway, and I'm not about to be shown up by athletes of a different sport.

I square my shoulders and narrow my eyes, assessing the playing field. I have to ignore both Sumi and Honor, who are making faces and catcalling aggressively. So unsportsmanlike. I take aim and then pop the ball into a careful arc in the air.

It splashes into a cup close to Honor, sending droplets of beer onto her arm. *BOOM!* Honor glares at me, brushes her wavy brown hair out of her face, and then picks up the cup, drinking *at* me without breaking eye contact. It's a lot. Then she slams it down and off to the side. "Game on."

Sumi takes the next shot, and it just barely grazes the rim of one cup. Then Colby takes her shot, and it misses entirely, hitting the corner of the table and rolling off into the bushes behind Honor and Sumi. "Oops!" she says, and laughs. I grin and pull her into a hug like she'd made the shot anyway. When she looks back at me, her smile is shy and sweet.

"Hey, lovebirds! Focus!" Sumi calls. Oh my God. We turn back to the table, just in time for the ball to plop into the red cup next to me. Colby, Honor, and Sumi look at me expectantly. Right. It's my turn. I grab the cup and bring it to my mouth. My nose wrinkles at the smell.

"It's just a little dirt!" Honor says, and I remember that the ball just fell off the table. Great.

"Thanks!" I say. Everyone else has taken their cups without issue. I'm not about to back down now. Plus, it isn't even that much beer—it barely fills the bottom of the cup. I finally pull my own mask off, take a deep breath, and down the amber liquid. Then promptly spit it out.

Good *God* that's disgusting.

"What's wrong?" Colby asks.

"Was there a bug?" Sumi asks.

"It's disgusting." I realize too late that it's probably the wrong thing to say. Honor starts laughing immediately.

"Dude," she says. "Have you never had *beer* before?"

Heat rises to my cheeks, and I suddenly feel like a toddler who's had an accident on the playground. Colby touches my arm. "You didn't have to drink it," she says. "We can get you water."

"Yeah, like a *baby*!" Honor calls.

"Don't be an ass," Sumi says, nudging her friend in the side. She comes around the table and, together with Colby, dumps the beer from our remaining red cups into one of the cups we'd put to the side.

"I'll take that!" Brian calls from the wicker table. Sumi hands it to him, while Colby grabs a water bottle from the cooler by the house door and fills each cup again. Then she winks at me. "This is better," she says. "Beer is, in fact, disgusting. Especially cheap beer."

"But they'll have an unfair advantage," Honor protests to Sumi. "We'll be drunk, and they'll be totally sober."

"Are you saying you can't handle a little bit of beer?"

Sumi raises an eyebrow. Colby was right—she, at least, is fun.

"Ugh, fine," Honor mutters. "But now, it's *really* on." She cracks her neck and fixes me with a thorough glare. I try to hold her gaze. This wasn't exactly what I had in mind for the evening, but like I said: It's my last day of high school. Why not be a little wild?

"Let's go," I say, and pitch the tiny ball forward. It makes another perfect arc through the air and lands with a plop in the cup in front of Honor. She frowns. I smirk.

Game on.

CHAPTER TEN

UNSURPRISINGLY, HONOR AND SUMI DO, IN fact, win.

They celebrate with an elaborate handshake before they both pop open two more cans of beer and challenge each other to a chugging contest. I don't know who won that one, because Colby is grabbing my hand and pulling me toward the door, through the house, and onto the front porch, where Bam-Bam has disappeared. I spot her hairy snout poking out from her house. Colby and I sit on the steps that lead to the screen door.

"I'm sorry Honor and Sumi are so . . . them," Colby says.

I shrug it off. "It ended up being sort of fun."

"Really?"

"Yeah! I learned a new game, discovered that beer is disgusting, and realized that I need to improve my aim if I'm ever going to redeem myself against two insane soccer jocks. All in all, I consider it a pretty successful evening."

That makes Colby laugh, which proves my point. It's been a *very* successful evening.

"Do you think it's shitty that we're out here?" she says suddenly.

I look at her in surprise. "What do you mean?"

"Like, that there's a whole quarantine mandate or whatever, and we're, like, outside, partying."

I think about Alexis's stern response to me this morning. "I don't know. I mean, like, most of us were masked, unless we were drinking. And we were outside. That's good, right?"

Colby nods, though she doesn't look convinced. It seems to occur to us at the same moment that neither of us have put our masks back over our mouths. We fix them silently. "My parents are super freaked out," she says quietly. "They've been taking really intense precautions, and now we have like an entire room of toilet paper."

I laugh a little. "I think my parents don't really know how to feel. It's been a lot, but we've been masking, and quarantining, and doing whatever they tell us to do.

Trying our best, I guess." Although Alexis, seeing me here now, would probably disagree.

"My uncle died," Colby whispers. She looks down. "In January, when no one knew what was happening. It was really sudden. We thought he had the flu, and then he was in the hospital for a week. He went home, and the next day, my aunt—his wife—called us, saying he'd died in his sleep. The doctors determined it was Covid."

"Oh my God," I gasp. "That's awful."

"We were really close." A few tears escape down her cheeks. She wipes them away. "He lived down the street from us, so I grew up with him. It was his birthday today."

"Colby . . ." I don't know what to say. I feel callous, and ignorant, like what I knew of the world was only a fraction of everything that was possible. I reach for her hand, and she lets me hold it. "I'm sorry," I say. Then—"My sister is in the hospital."

Colby looks up at me in surprise, but I shake my head quickly. "Not from Covid. From, uh . . . she tried to kill herself."

It's the first time I've let myself say the words. *My sister tried to kill herself.* If I'm supposed to feel lighter or something, I don't. The words just twist into a knot inside my chest and stay there.

Colby's fingers tighten around mine. The pressure is comforting. "That's awful. Is she okay?"

"I mean, she's alive," I say. "But I don't know if she's okay. Or, I don't know if she's going to be okay. She's in an induced coma because of the drugs she took."

"Oh, Tia." Colby brings my hand to her still-covered mouth, and the soft paper of her mask brushes against my skin. "I'm so sorry."

"It's just crazy." I keep talking, but I don't know why. "Like, I feel bad about being out here, but also, I feel like we could die at any moment anyway. Either from getting killed like George Floyd, or from Covid, or because, I don't know, we feel like it one day. It's just like . . . I don't know, like we should try to live while we can, I guess."

She lays her head on my shoulder. "Yeah. I feel like I should be home, but my mom can't stop crying. Some days she's okay, and other days, she just breaks down, saying *my baby brother, my baby brother*." She sniffles. "I think I'm a bad daughter."

"I don't think you're a bad daughter," I say. "I think you're just trying to give your mom space. You can give her a big hug when you get home."

My shoulder vibrates, and I think she's chuckling. I hope she is. "My dad is at home," she says. "He knows I went out."

"He doesn't mind?"

"Well, I think he probably does mind. But he's prioritizing Mom today. I mean, that's why they finally let me keep working at Paw House too. Because, on the one hand, they're terrified, but on the other hand . . ."

"Your mom is grieving," I say.

"We all are," she whispers. "And we can't do it if we're all stuck within the same four walls, screaming at each other every day."

I put my head on hers, and she nuzzles deeper into my neck. I think of what my family would do, if the worst were to happen with Mel. That's why I'm really at Alexis's house, after all. To get away from my parents' suffocating sadness. To get away from *my* suffocating sadness. And now I wonder if that's why Alexis invited me over too. Because the person keeping her sane had to leave and *she* didn't want to be alone. We all need different things in different ways . . . Suddenly, I'm not so scandalized by the existence of her pandemic puppy. Maybe, as much as Alexis is taking care of Poirot, he's been taking care of her too. Maybe I have been, too, just by being there with her.

Except I'm not with her now.

Guilt gnaws at my chest, but a sudden cascade of rough grunts erupts from beside us, distracting me from my thoughts. We look over at Bam-Bam. "Oh my

God," Colby says. "Is she dreaming?" Bam-Bam's full head is peaking out of her little house now, and her eyes are blinking open and shut rapidly as the grunts slow and intensify in steady rhythms.

"I have never seen a pig dream before," I say with genuine awe. "That's pretty cool."

"It must be nice," Colby said. "To be a pig."

"Well, this one. I imagine most of them who make it to a city like this are probably eaten." Wow. Why the hell would I say that?

I fully expect Colby to pull away from me in disgust, but she just releases a heavy sigh. "Good point," she says. "In that case, dream on, little Bam-Bam. You deserve all the peace in the world." Then she nuzzles back into my shoulder. "Sorry," she says when she's done. "My nose itched."

"I did not mind. You can do it again, if you want."

"Oh yeah?"

"One hundred percent."

"Why are you so cute?"

"I—" I don't know what to say to that. "Uh." She's looking up at me now, and I think maybe she wants me to kiss her, but I'm not sure. Her eyes dart to my mouth, and I think that's probably a good indication. Forgetting that I'm wearing a mask, I dip my head forward.

"Hey, Beer Baby." A heavy hand falls on my other shoulder. Honor is standing above us, a jacket slung over her shoulders, and a mask covering her face. "Good game."

Between the almost kiss, that dreadful nickname, and the surprising show of camaraderie, I'm feeling too disoriented to respond. Honor doesn't bother to wait. She steps past us and then turns to Colby, offering up her fist. Colby taps it with her own. She doesn't look the least bit upset. In fact, she seems highly amused. I can't imagine what Honor must be like at work. I'm sure it keeps the days interesting.

"Listen, a few of us are headed up to Pacific Beach right now. Thought it might be nice to have a little beach bonfire. Do you want to come?"

Colby and I share a quick look, and the words are out of my mouth before I can stop them. "One hundred percent."

CHAPTER ELEVEN

THE OCEAN IS BEAUTIFUL. THERE'S A FULL moon tonight, and it's reflecting off the surface of the water, creating a pool of light that rolls toward us, rippling over the waves. The water laps against the sand in a gentle rhythm and I breathe in tandem. I can understand why Colby would want to live out here. It's a natural sort of peace, undisturbed by the concerns of the shore.

She's sitting beside me. Her knees are drawn up to her chest, and her arms are wrapped around her legs. Her bare feet dig into the sand and she's wearing my jacket, even though she claimed she didn't need it. The night breeze brushes against my skin, but there's warmth in my chest that I haven't felt in a long time.

It feels light and glowing, like in this moment and this moment alone, life is a promise fulfilled.

Behind us, a fire crackles in a pit surrounded by people I met an hour ago. I hear them laughing; I know some of them are drinking. A few people are wearing masks, but most of us aren't anymore, including Colby and me, and I hope that's okay. I hope in the sea of teenage mistakes that this is a little one that can be forgiven by whoever keeps score.

Another breeze, and this time a shiver I can't hide runs through me. Colby looks at me and glares. "Okay," she says, "I'm warm now. Put your jacket back on."

"I'm fine!" I try to insist, but she's already shifting it off and putting it around me.

"I don't want to be responsible for you dying of hypothermia," she says.

"Why not?" I say. "I'd rather that, than disease or death by cop."

She sighs and I kick myself for ruining the mood. Again. I'm usually so good at biting my tongue, but it's like it bursts out of me at the very moments I should shut up. But then she scoots a little closer. Lays her head on my shoulder, and I put my arm around hers.

"We can both be warm," she says instead, and like that, the trance we were in begins again.

Swallowing my fear, I tug her a little closer to me

and place a kiss on her forehead. Her skin is chilled by the ocean air. She reaches up around my neck and draws my lips to hers instead. They're warm, and gentle, and soft. I sigh into her mouth, and she takes it as an invitation. The pressure on my neck increases and she's holding me closer, so I hold *her* closer, and then I can't tell who's holding on to who tighter, but it feels like we're the waves, pulled by gravity, pulling in light, and promising a world beneath that is vaster and more full of life than anyone on Earth has ever managed to uncover.

Our foreheads stay pressed together even as our mouths break apart, and as we breathe, there's a song in my throat.

"What are you humming?" Colby asks.

"'*Be my lover / I'll cover you,*'" I rasp out, the tune mangled by my lack of breath, and general inability to sing.

"What's that?"

I laugh. "It's from the musical *Rent.*"

She covers her mouth in mock surprise. "Oh my God," she says. "I have a crush on a theater nerd."

I laugh, loud, and she laughs with me, burying her head into my chest to muffle the sounds. Then I realize what she said. "You have a crush on me?"

She turns her head and looks at me incredulously. "I thought that was obvious."

I grin and bend my head toward her again, my gaze dancing between her beautiful brown eyes and her lips. "I guess," I whisper.

"Hey, Beer Baby!"

"Oh, for the love of . . ." I pull away as Colby starts to giggle again. I turn my body toward the firepit, where Honor is now standing, facing me. "What?"

"We're doing a group trudge to the bathroom," Honor says. "Safety and whatever. Do you need to go?" I'm about to say no, when I realize that it's dark, and late, and if this is my chance to take care of my biological necessities, I should probably take it.

"We should go," Colby mutters with a sigh.

"Fine," I respond sullenly. She stands before I do and then offers me her hand, pulling me up with surprising strength. We walk arm in arm toward Honor and the two other people waiting beside her: Marcus, the future vet, and a Latine enby who introduces themself as Nelson.

Honor leads the way to the boardwalk and toward a place advertised as a "sports bar and grill." Although it's past one A.M., it's bustling with patrons, several of whom are sitting outside, laughing and chatting loudly beneath brightly lit yellow canopies, as a row of TVs inside blare something about fouls and trades and other snippets I can barely pick up over the general noise. Absolutely no one is wearing a mask.

A white woman is standing at a host station outside the entrance to the bar. Honor tries to walk past her, but the woman stops her with a firm smile. "Hello," she says, stepping into Honor's path. She eyes the group of us, and I realize for the first time how young we all must look. "This bar is twenty-one and older. Can I see your IDs?"

Honor frowns and looks back at us. We all look away. None of us are twenty-one.

"Um," Nelson pipes up from behind. "We just have to use the bathroom. Is that okay?"

"No, sorry. Bathroom is for patrons only," the hostess says. Her tone is apologetic, but her body language suggests she couldn't possibly care less.

"Aww, c'mon, sugar," a white man shouts from the table beside her. He's sitting with two other white guys, who are smirking to themselves. His face is ruddy as he leans back in his chair, an arm draped across the back seat of one of his buddies. "Let 'em in. They're having a bad couple weeks. Haven't you seen the news?"

I duck my face, hoping I'm misinterpreting his point, but he keeps talking. "George Floyd is dead. Black Lives Matter, right? At least let those two in." He points to Colby and me. Marcus must be too pale for him to clock as Black.

“Whoa,” one of his friends, the man with curly blond hair, says to the table. “They’re holding hands. Are they lesbians?” Then, louder, for the whole boardwalk to hear. “Are you lesbians?”

“We should go,” I say to Colby, but the hostess is moving aside.

“Go ahead,” she says to all of us. “Just be quick about it.”

Honor looks at us again, and then we all shuffle in, heads bowed. Absently, I notice that no one is wearing masks inside either. Nelson hesitates outside the men’s room, and Marcus pats them on the shoulder. “I’ll go in first.” He pops in, then out. “All clear.” Nelson thanks him, and they go in together as Honor, Colby, and I go inside the other restroom.

“Was that guy being an ally or was he being an ass?” I ask once we’re all at the sink, washing our hands.

“Maybe both,” Honor says. “I suppose that’s possible.”

“Or he’s just drunk,” Colby says. We agree that’s probably the most likely scenario. Outside the bathrooms, Nelson and Marcus are already waiting for us. Unfortunately, so is the drunk guy. He’s leaning against the wall, and when he sees Colby and me, he smiles.

"Hey," he says. "So, since I helped y'all get inside, I thought maybe I could get a nice thank-you." He leans toward me. "Like a kiss or something."

"Okay, we're going now," Honor says, pulling my arm, but the guy grabs my other hand.

"Come on," he says. "I'm not asking for much."

"Let her go," Nelson says, just as Colby pries the guy's hand off mine. His glassy red eyes blink and his hand shoots back out, landing against Marcus, who has moved to shield us both.

"Hey, fuck you, man," he says to Marcus. "You of all people should understand. I'm just asking for a little kindness in return. They needed help, I helped them." He's shouting this as we're hurrying away, still under the apparent impression that Marcus is white, like him. "That's why you people keep getting killed," he shouts at our retreating backs.

It must've only taken a few seconds, but it feels like centuries pass when we finally make it back outside. The blond guy who asked if we were lesbians is half standing, half sitting, like he was about to come inside. He must've heard the shouting. "Shit, I was just joking," he says to his other friend. "I didn't think he was actually going to go in there." That friend is still comfortably sitting at the table, laughing like this situation is the funniest thing he's ever experienced, but the blond glances between us and the door with a look of utter bewilderment.

"Y'all okay?" The hostess calls as we pass, but we keep walking, the pack of us pressed in together like penguins to keep from dying of cold. We're moving fast, away from the bar and soon back onto the sand, our steps silent, hoping that no one is following us, that no one else has noticed us, that the targets we didn't realize were on our backs diminish against the retreating light of the boardwalk.

Thirty minutes later, Colby double-parks next to a black Honda Civic in front of Alexis's apartment. The car has a small yellow sticker in the corner of its back window that says BABY ON BOARD. Above it, on white printer paper, are the words *Black Babies Matter*, handwritten in bold black ink. I stare at it as we sit in Colby's car, as silent as we have been since leaving the beach. Colby reaches for my knee. "Are you okay?"

It's the question of the year, apparently. I want to say something snarky, and stupid, but I'm not the only one living this nightmare. Instead, I put my hand on top of hers. "Are you?"

She gives a weak smile. "We'll see."

Yeah. That sounds about right.

"Thanks for driving me home," I say, because that seems like the most neutral follow-up.

"I'm sorry I invited you out tonight," Colby says. She's looking down and frowning, and then all of sudden she's crying. "I'm really sorry."

"You didn't do anything wrong. It was a good night, all things considered."

"Really?"

"Yeah," I say. To prove my point, I reach for her chin and pull her mouth toward me. If nothing else, kissing Colby seems like the most valuable skill I could have ever hoped to discover. She kisses me back, and for a second, the world seems right again. But there are still tears in her eyes.

"I was really scared," she whispers.

"Yeah. Me too." I don't want to keep talking, but my mouth moves before I can stop it. "It felt like . . . like it was the tee up. Like, what you hear about on TV, you know. Everything starts out normal, and then—"

"And then you're dead." Colby laughs and the wind chimes sound brittle and hollow. I want to kiss the sweetness back into them. I try to. She lets me.

"I'm glad you're not dead," I say, and she smiles. A real smile.

"I'm glad you're not dead too."

It shouldn't be romantic; it really shouldn't. But it feels almost as good as I imagine it does to say *I love you* for the first time. Like someone sees you, understands you, and wants you anyway. It makes me feel like I'm not broken, just a little messed up. And that's okay. It's going to be okay.

We're still making googly eyes at each other when I glance at my phone. I'm not expecting anything, but I've been checking it periodically throughout the night, making sure Alexis hasn't woken up suddenly and frantically called the police. Thankfully, everything's been silent on the home front. Until now.

On my screen is Alexis's smiling face beneath the most alarming words in human history.

Incoming call.

CHAPTER TWELVE

I GIVE MYSELF FIVE MINUTES. TO KISS COLBY goodbye. To walk to the front door. To breathe, nice and slow. I remind myself that Alexis is my sister, not my parent, and then I remember that Mom told me to look after her, that I was supposed to be making things easier for her, not harder. That Mel broke, and I've been worried that Alexis would too. When did I stop worrying? Why would I let myself stop worrying? What a silly privilege I thought I had. But I breathe—one, two, three. I open the door with the spare key I've been using to walk Poirot. Alexis is sitting on the couch, looking tired. Poirot is lying beside her, his body rolled into a little ball.

"Hey," I say.

Alexis looks at me, and I'm struck by the fire in her eyes. I don't think I've ever seen her so angry before.

"Look," I say. "I know you told me not to go out, but–"

She holds up a hand. Breathes too. Then: "Mel is awake."

INTERLUDE #3

I DON'T REALLY LIKE COFFEE. IT TASTES LIKE bitterness and despair topped with sugar, but Alexis and Mel both drink it like it's the nectar of the gods. It might be because they've both been drinking it since they were kids, but by the time I came along, our mom realized that even *un poco cafecito* can stunt your growth, so I was never encouraged to try it.

Another one of those "baby of the family" perks, I guess.

But last year, I got an internship at a local software company. I don't have any interest in software or communications, but I had to get a summer job, and at the time, I thought I might have a crush on Ramón, this cute Dominican boy from my calculus class. He smiled at me sometimes, and I thought that counted as charming. I didn't get any butterflies, but I thought that if he liked me, I might as well like him back. Somehow, though, that translated into me wanting to avoid him at all costs, and I knew he worked at an ice cream shop, which was the only place within walking distance that was hiring for the summer.

So, I searched online and found a marketing internship. After asking my parents if they'd be okay to drive me, I applied and interviewed, and miraculously, the company hired me. Bam, an easy seventeen dollars an hour, and no Ramón to run from—or, er, be distracted by. (This should have been a big indicator that I was gay, but hey. You live and learn.)

When my first day of work came, I woke up at seven in the morning and went downstairs. In the kitchen, waiting for me, were Mel and Alexis. Alexis, in her khaki capris and striped blue-and-white button-down blouse, was holding a Snoopy balloon that said CONGRATULATIONS, and Mel, in a pair of black baggy jeans and an old Tegan and Sara concert tee that showed her midriff, was standing beside her. In each of Mel's hands was one bag of coffee grounds.

"Congratulations," my sisters said in unison when I entered the kitchen.

"For what?" I muttered, still blinking sleep out of my eyes.

"For your first grown-up job!"

"It's an internship."

"Close enough," Alexis said. She pulled me into a hug, and it occurred to me that she, unlike Mel, did not live that close.

"Did you drive here from San Diego?"

"Yup! I left around five. Traffic wasn't too bad." She handed me the Snoopy balloon as Mel lifted the two bags of coffee into my line of sight.

"Since this is your first sort-of job, we thought we would indoctrinate you into the family tradition of overcaffeinated coping mechanisms."

"That sounds horrifying."

"It is! But, like, with love. Okay, so, this one is a French vanilla dark roast from my favorite coffee shop around the corner," Mel said, lifting her left hand.

"And this," Alexis said, pointing to the beans in Mel's right hand, "is a light hazelnut blend from *my* favorite coffee shop in San Diego."

"Which one do you want to try?" Mel asked.

I peered at both bags, without a clue to guide me. "Um. What if I try both?"

"GREAT answer," Alexis said. "Let's start with one for the morning, and then we'll prep one for the afternoon, when it's two P.M. and you're desperate to escape the confines of your corporate prison cell."

"You are not selling this well," Mel responded, smiling. "Although, that is an accurate description."

They corralled me toward the corner of the kitchen that held the coffee grinder and demonstrated how to measure and grind Alexis's light hazelnut coffee blend. Then they poured it into the French press and covered it with the hot water they'd already had boiling on the stove. As we waited for the coffee to brew, we got started on grinding Mel's French vanilla dark roast. Soon, the kitchen was filled with a smooth and heavy scent, like clean smoke. You breathe in something bold and brooding and breathe out feeling as if the ground has risen to meet your feet. It was solid, and whole.

"So," Alexis said when there were two to-go mugs of coffee on the counter before us. She was eager, bright eyes shimmering like they do when she's feeling competitive. Like they do when she's feeling happy. Mel was more relaxed, as always, leaning against the counter with her arms crossed and eyebrows raised. She looked even shorter than usual, though she's still taller than me by half an inch. With medium brown skin like Mom and tight curls like Dad, she's the middle child through and through. That day, her hair was big and poofy, down to her shoulders and covering part of her eyes. She pushed it out of the way to give Alexis a pointed look—one that clearly said, *You're doing the most*. But she was still smiling, because we all know Alexis's joy is infectious.

What Mel doesn't know is that hers is too.

So, I smiled, because they were smiling, and because there before me was a crowning ceremony no one prepared me for, a tradition that didn't exist before my sisters decided it should. I sipped one cup and then the other.

The answer, in the end, was that both cups tasted like dirt. It would take much more milk and much, much, *much* more sugar until, finally, we determined that Mel had the slight edge up on coffee choices.

"Booyah," Mel said, dropping a pretend mic as Alexis pouted.

"It doesn't count. I think Tia might just hate coffee."

"Sure," Mel said. "But she hates mine slightly less, and that . . . that makes all the difference."

"Don't quote Robert Frost at me."

"Or what? Does poetry offend you?"

The two started bickering at a reference I didn't understand until English class this year, but I watched as they both reached for the mugs of coffee they had made me. I don't think they noticed, but Mel took Alexis's preferred coffee, and Alexis took

Mel's. They each sipped and continued to bicker, which confirmed to me that there wasn't the slightest difference between them.

Then they turned to me at the same time, like a clock had rung in both their minds. "You gotta get dressed, sis!" Mel exclaimed.

"Can't be late on your first day!" Alexis said.

I balked at them. "If I'm late, whose fault is that?"

And then it was my turn to bicker with them as they ushered me out of the kitchen. I showered, got dressed, and they piled into the car with me, Mel in the driver's seat and Alexis behind me as I took the passenger seat, and I thought to myself that I may not have loved the coffee, but I have never loved my sisters more.

CHAPTER THIRTEEN

I THINK I UNDERSTAND WHAT ALEXIS HAS JUST said, but the words feel garbled, like I'm hearing them through water. "What?"

"Mel is awake," she repeats.

My face breaks into a grin. "That's—that's great!" Alexis nods and looks up at the ceiling. She swallows, tears pricking her eyes. "I mean . . . it is, right?"

Alexis nods again and then shakes her head. "Yeah. But we can't go to see her, because you went out with—how many people?"

I don't understand what she's saying. What does that have to do with . . .

"Was everyone masked? Were you all six feet apart? Did you know any of them? Do you know what the goddamn point of quarantine is? Because the point,

Tia, the *point* is to keep each other safe, to make sure people with bad immune systems aren't more likely to *die*, and do you know how strong someone's immune system is when they've just woken up from an induced coma after a drug overdose?"

Reality sinks in. I slump against the door. "Not great."

"Not fucking great," Alexis agreed. "So, we're staying here, inside the apartment, for the next two weeks, before we can see Mel."

"But I . . . it's no different than if there were like, a protest, or whatever. If I had gone to one of those, wouldn't it be the same difference?"

Alexis laughs and wipes her eyes. "Maybe. But you didn't go to a protest, Tia. At least then you'd be doing something that . . . that matters. You were just horny and stupid and snuck out in the middle of the night to party with strangers and a girl you met two days ago."

"Having fun matters," I mutter to myself, but even I know that it's a ridiculous response. *Having fun matters*? I might as well make a print and sell it on Etsy with a hashtag.

"I can't with you right now," Alexis whispers. "I'm going back to bed. I'll talk to you in the morning." She picks up Poirot and walks away without sparing me another glance.

Slowly, I walk to the couch and drop onto it, feeling lower than I've ever felt in my life. There's a pressure behind my eyes, but I push it away by picking up my phone instead. Colby texted me.

Home safe.

I start to reply, but then I think better of it. I open my texts to Drew instead.

Mel's awake.

I don't expect him to respond yet, given that it's nearly four in the morning, but soon enough, his name pops up as my phone starts to buzz. I answer without hesitation.

"Hey," I say.

"Hi," he says. "That's great, that Mel's awake. Do you know how she's feeling?"

"No," I say. "Alexis just told me, but she's pissed because I snuck out."

He gasps. "You what? Snuck out? YOU?"

I chuckle a little. "I know, right? Three days in San Diego and I'm already a rebel."

"I'm scared of you," he says jokingly. "But okay, that is new. What were you sneaking out for?"

I pause, realizing that now I have to tell Drew about

Colby. For a second, I consider switching topics, but not only would that be suspicious, I don't even know what I would switch topics to. I decide to brave it and just tell him the truth. "Uh, I went out with some people I met. To a party. It was outdoors, though." I add this last part quickly, lest he judge me like Alexis already has.

"Wow, that's super unlike you," he says. He's silent for a minute. "Honestly, I'm kind of surprised because I thought you were scared of being in a group of people. Like, I thought that's why you were trippin' about going to those protests with me."

Oh. I mean, he's not wrong. A big group of people shouting and chanting isn't exactly my idea of a good time. "I mean . . . it wasn't a big party."

I hear him shift. "Nah, it's cool, I get it. I guess I just figured that, like . . . I don't know, maybe you were worried about being around a lot of people and then being around Mel."

His words feel like a screw digging into my skin. "Yeah," I say.

He waits for me to keep talking. When I don't, he tries gallantly to change the subject. "Well," he says slowly. "I guess it was some party, then. Good people? Anybody cute?"

I perk up a little. This is the perfect opportunity to introduce Colby. After all, he asked! "Yeah, actually.

There's this girl I met a couple days ago, and we hit it off. She invited me to the party tonight."

"Oh," he says. "Damn." He follows it with a shallow laugh. "I was kind of joking."

"Oh," I say.

More silence.

"Um," he starts. "Listen, I'm gonna go. I'm glad Mel is awake. Tell me how she's doing, okay?"

"Drew, wait—"

But he hangs up, and I'm left with silence and a dam of tears behind my eyes. They're begging to fall. I bet it would feel good too. But the problem is, if I let myself cry, I don't know if I'll be able to stop. So, instead, I stare at the ceiling, breathe, and wait until sleep takes me away.

CHAPTER FOURTEEN

I WAKE UP THE NEXT MORNING WITH MY mouth full of curse words.

Alexis *was not lying* about the parakeets. They are loud, incessant, and woke me up as soon as the sun began to consider rising. I've barely heard them the last couple days, but today it's as if they live inside the walls.

Ah. Alexis's door is already open. That's why.

I try to spend my first waking moments pretending I'm a Zen monk, but no: I hate the parakeets, and Parakeet Man, and whoever thought domesticating birds and allowing more than one to exist in a single home was a sane and legal possibility. If and when Poirot banshee-screams again, it will only be the most rational revenge.

Once I accept that the parakeets will continue to

slowly drain me of my will to live, I peel myself off the couch and let my feet find the floor. Suddenly, a phone is shoved in front of my face.

"It's Mel," Alexis says. I look up and she's already fully dressed, a cup of coffee in her hands. I recognize the bold smell as she walks back toward her room and closes her door. I take it all is not yet forgiven. At least the parakeets' chatter disappears with her.

"Hello?" I say. It's with a brightness I don't feel, but something pushes me to be normal. To act like talking to Mel today isn't any different than it has been for the last seventeen years of my life. Because it isn't. It shouldn't be.

A scratchy voice greets me on the other end. "Hey, sis." Suddenly, the world melts away. The only thing that matters is the sound of my other sister's voice, quiet and shallow, but living all the same.

"Hi," I say, and that's when it happens. The tears. They come, fast, and suddenly I can't see or speak. I'm not even sure I'm breathing. I hold the phone tighter to my ear and my eyes blur, my cheeks feeling hot and wet as I choke back sobs.

"It's okay," I hear Mel say, and then suddenly, I feel arms around me, pulling me close, and a hand on my back, rotating in small, soothing circles.

"It's okay," I hear again, and this time it's Alexis,

rocking me slowly as she rubs my back. She sighs and kisses my forehead as she pulls the phone away from me. "You there?" she asks Mel.

"I'm here," I hear Mel say, since Alexis is close enough for me to listen in. "I guess it wasn't my time."

"That's not funny," Alexis says.

"Sorry," Mel responds.

They keep talking, though about what, I can't imagine. My head hurts now, and so does my face and my throat. Alexis keeps holding me. When I'm able to breathe again, she gives me a questioning look. I nod, and she hands the phone back.

"Hi," I say again.

"Hi," Mel says. "Are you okay?"

"Are you?"

"I'm okay. I promise."

"But how can you promise?" The heat in my face and cheeks and throat comes out in my words. "You overdosed—on purpose."

"Tia," Alexis says, but I'm not done.

"You—you can't say you promise you're okay when you're not. Are you . . . are you going to see a therapist, again, after this?"

"I've been seeing a therapist," Mel answers.

"Okay, so, that's not helping. Maybe you need to find a new one."

"*Tia*," Alexis tries again, but I stand and walk away with the phone still against my ear. I need answers, and I need Mel to have them.

"I know you're upset," Mel says. She coughs a little. "And I know you were scared. I'm sorry."

"You don't need to be sorry," I say, although I'm not sure that's true. Maybe she *should* be sorry. After all, a bunch of people were dying because of the pandemic, and because of trigger-happy cops, and here she was, trying to kill *herself*. It was thoughtless, and *terrifying*. "We should come up with a plan, though. For the next time this happens. Because it could happen again."

"Okay, sis," Mel says. She sighs, and I can hear that she's tired, but I don't want to let up or let her go.

"What's the . . . What's next? Are you at the hospital or at home?"

"Hospital," she says. "For the rest of the day, at least. Just so they can monitor any changes. Then I can go home."

"Are Mom and Dad with you? Or Olivia?"

"No. They've asked for people to stay home. Olivia is gonna pick me up."

Right. It makes sense that she'd go home to her apartment with her girlfriend. Still, I'm surprised my parents haven't insisted that she stay in her childhood room so they can keep an eye on her. Maybe they want to support her independence. I'm not sure that's the best idea, though. I'm about to say so, when I see that Alexis is standing nearby, her arms crossed as she watches me like she wants to make sure I'm not about to say more out-of-pocket things. I guess that means I have to choose my words more carefully. Fine.

"Um." I lick my lips, swallow the lump in my throat. Wait for the shaky breaths to pass. "I missed you," I say finally.

"I missed you too, kiddo." Mel says it with a whisper, and for the first time, I let myself imagine what she must look like, a young woman on the brink of death and back again. Maybe she's lying in one of the hospital beds you see on TV, in a bland hospital gown. I wonder if her skin is paler than it should be—maybe pallid is the word?—and I wonder how long it will take for the color to return to her cheeks. I wonder if anyone touched her hair—if they were allowed to, or if that's against hospital protocol or something. If it wasn't, would anyone even know how to? Like Dad and me, she has tight coils that need a decent amount of care. Mel's a pro at making her hair look shiny and moisturized. Buoyant. I wonder if her hair is flat and crunchy now. Lifeless and tangled, like disparate limbs buried in sand.

If she's propped up, maybe there's a tray of bland food in front of her, like a carton of apple juice and another of apple sauce. I wonder if they know she's vegetarian, and if they gave her salmon instead of meat loaf, because people do that sometimes when they think vegetarians eat fish. I guess some do, but Mel doesn't. I wonder if she can drink water from a cup now, or if it'll feel weird, since she's been getting hydration from a tube. I wonder if she can drink coffee soon.

"Can I bring you a coffee soon?" I ask, and she laughs, soft and willowy, like air passing through a hollow tube. I don't hate the sound, but I don't love it either. It doesn't sound as strong as it should be. As strong as Mel is.

"Yes, please," she says. "It's the first thing I asked for, and they said no."

"That sucks," I say, and then she sighs again, because she's tired. I know she's tired. I look at Alexis. And even though I don't want her to take the phone, she does, and I feel like a little kid again. Alexis, the resident parental figure, taking over while I become small and feeble.

Useless.

Alexis promises Mel that we'll see her before long, while I put on my shoes and head out the door. It's only when I reach the bottom of the steps that I realize I didn't take my own phone, or a wallet, or anything of value. And that, even if I had, I shouldn't go anywhere.

Can't speak to anyone. Not if I want to see Mel anytime soon. We have to be "quarantined," and that means being alone. Isolated.

I sit on the last step instead and lay my head on knees. I guess I'll have to be okay with my own company for now.

CHAPTER FIFTEEN

A FEW MINUTES LATER, I HEAR THE DOOR PULL open. Footsteps follow, and soon Alexis sits behind me, a step above. She doesn't say anything. Instead, she waits, humming a tune I don't recognize at first. Alexis doesn't think so, but she's got the same talents as Mom and Dad—that musical sensibility about her, where emotions turn to melodies when she's not thinking too hard about them. Mom doesn't sing for a living, the way Dad makes music, but that's how they met. At karaoke, at a bar, a millennia ago. Dad says he heard her sing Brandy's "Have You Ever," and that's when he knew she was the one.

Alexis inherited their combined musical prowess, and when she was twelve or thirteen, Dad tried to convince her to join a local singing competition, but she refused. She likes things orderly, and the world of a musician seemed too chaotic to her. Like Mom, she wanted something steady, secure. Singing was fun, but it was personal; something just for her.

I look back at her now, and she's looking around, slowly rocking side to side to her own humming. I can tell it's comforting her as much as it's meant to comfort me. In fact, it strikes me that this is the first time I've heard her hum all weekend. That's a good sign.

And even though she's been working from the kitchen table or the coffee table or sometimes her bedroom, today she's got on black slacks and a blue blouse with ruffle sleeves. Her hair, with far looser curls than mine or Mel's, has been brushed back into a ponytail. Her nails are clean, painted with a nice nude color, and she's got a splash of gloss on her lips. She's even wearing a pair of gold studs, which I know she put on this morning, because she doesn't sleep in jewelry except her wedding ring.

She looks so put together, my big sister. But if I look closer, I can see the circles beneath her eyes. I can see that the cuticle of her left thumb is looking haggard, like she's been picking at it, methodically, day after day. It's such a small detail that it's easy to miss. But I know that Alexis picks at her nails when she's stressed. Once, when she was a senior in high school and I was still in kindergarten, I remember her screaming bloody murder because she'd accidentally torn the skin beneath the nail of her pinkie while studying for finals. I was the closest to her room, so I got her a Band-Aid and kissed it, like Mom and Dad did for me when I got a boo-boo.

Now I reach for her hand. She lets me, and our fingers clasp while she continues to hum. I realize I know the melody. "*It's like cranes in the sky . . .*" It's a song from years ago, by Solange, about feeling an endless, melancholic pain. A haunting sadness that seems impossible to exorcise—like construction cranes that litter the sky, promising reinvention while blocking out the sun.

It feels particularly apt. Not just for today, either, but for what feels like much, much longer.

Alexis continues to hum, and I lay my head on her knee. We stay like that until the door of the first-floor apartment opens. Parakeet Man walks out. He's got a black trash bag in his hand and a parakeet I haven't seen before—this one a deep blue and green—on his shoulder. Alexis and I both freeze when he walks past us, and he stops, his drawn face looking particularly gaunt and unforgiving.

"My window is open," he says slowly. "I can hear you humming."

It wasn't even that loud, but okay. Alexis doesn't say

sorry, though. She just stares back at him. The hand that's holding mine tightens.

"She likes it," he says. The parakeet bounces her little feathery head up and down like she agrees.

Then he keeps walking, toward the alleyway past the stairs.

Alexis and I exchange a look of utter surprise and then break out into belly laughter that seems to soothe our spirits. "Oh, that reminds me," I say. "I don't hear Poirot dying of neglect."

"Ah," Alexis says. "I gave him peanut butter in a little toy. He's occupied . . . for now. But we should probably head back in." She cocks her head, and I stand, offering her my hand.

Inside, she removes the toy from Poirot's desperate paws so she can prepare breakfast for him, and as she does, I clean up the living room from the clothes and things I've left strewn about. "So," I say, as I settle back down. "I didn't actually pack enough clothes for two weeks . . ."

"Yeah," Alexis says as she adjusts a pillow on the couch and puts her laptop on the coffee table. "So, since Mel is staying with her girlfriend, we can probably go back to Mom and Dad's and quarantine there, so we're not too far."

I take in a grateful breath. "Good."

"Yeah," she says again. "Also . . . I was maybe a little too zealous last night. I have no idea if going to the grocery store is any different than going to a party, even if I was masked. I do know it was *necessary*"—she gives me a pointed look—"but it could still be enough to warrant quarantine around a person recovering from bad health. So, I don't know." She leans back into her seat on the couch. "Speaking of going home . . . have you talked to Drew recently?"

"Oh." I groan and cover my face. "Yeah. I told him about Colby."

She raises an eyebrow. "How did that go?"

"Terribly."

"I'm sorry." She places a hand on my shoulder. "He'll come around."

"I guess." We're silent for a moment, my head still lodged between my hands. Then I dare a peek from between my fingers. "Are you going to tell Mom and Dad that I snuck out?"

She sighs and pulls her laptop onto her lap, sparing me an irritated glance that I still clock as fond and sisterly. "No. I'm not a narc, and you're alive and well. Plus, we all do stupid things when we have crushes."

"I don't believe you've ever done something stupid for a crush."

At that, a mischievous smile slowly spreads across

her lips. "You'd be surprised. I snuck out once for a boy I met on MySpace. We went to elementary school together, and he found me when we were in eleventh grade. When I tell you he *grew up*. Oof." She fans herself and I laugh.

"How'd that go?"

"Eh. He was not a great kisser. And I was lucky–I actually did know who he was, so I'm not condoning meeting strangers online."

I roll my eyes. "Obviously. I met Colby at the park."

"Right," she says. "Speaking of, Poirot does need to go out again, since he just ate." She waggles her eyebrows, and I hop up to grab my phone.

"Wear a mask," she says sternly. "And stay six feet apart. *Please.*"

"Aye-aye, captain!"

"I think he's starting to disobey me on purpose." Colby and I are standing in the clearing of the dog park now, far away from the other pet parents, and several feet from each other, just like I promised Alexis, and we're also both wearing masks. It's similar to the first night we hung out together, training Poirot and Grim, except this time, there are people around us throwing Frisbees or otherwise enjoying the late morning with their dogs. Poirot, meanwhile, is still on his leash, and sitting in front of me on the grass. He is staring me straight in the eyes as he continues chewing on the stick I just told him to drop.

Colby stifles a giggle with one hand, her other hand wrapped loosely on Grim's leash. "Dogs do that sometimes," she responds, "if they know you're going to give them a treat to get them to do the *right* thing."

I glare at Poirot. "So, you're actually an evil genius, huh?" He continues chewing. Pointedly. I reach down and scratch his ear and then tug the stick from his mouth. He growls and tugs it back. "Seriously?" Even though he's tiny, his little puppy teeth are like razors. He uses them to his advantage and positions the stick more firmly in his mouth. Then he gives a playful bow and darts away with it. Thankfully, since he's still on his leash, he doesn't go very far. He just runs as far as the leash will let him and as soon as it tugs him back, he turns and goes in the other direction. Eventually, he settles on running in a circle with me as the center point.

"This is useless," I mutter. Grim grunts like he agrees. Colby bends down to rub his neck, and he nuzzles his nose against her face, just as Poirot finally decides now is the perfect time to launch himself at both of them. Before I can react, Colby falls over as Poirot climbs her chest, attempting to cover her face in puppy kisses even as Colby holds him back, giggling. "Oh no, Poirot!" I start to move toward them, and Colby puts her hand up.

"It's okay," she says. "He's fine. He's much smaller than Grim." She nuzzles Poirot's face and then stands up with him still wiggling in her arms. She picks up the stick he dropped nearby and gives it a small throw. He runs toward it and then lies down, chewing on it happily. Again.

"So," Colby says. The joyful crinkles in the corners of her eyes disappear. I already told her the good news about my sister. Now we have to talk about the bad news. "When are you going back to Irvine?"

"When Alexis is off of work tonight. Her husband, Houston, will be home at like three A.M., so he'll handle Poirot."

"Ah," she says. "That's good. I mean, if you needed a sitter or something, I'm sure my parents wouldn't mind, but that's good." She looks off to the side and doesn't say anything else. After a beat, she pulls down her mask and rubs her face, like the paper was beginning to stifle her.

I clear my throat, my heart thudding loudly in my chest. "Can we, like, keep talking?"

Her lips pull to the side, causing her nose to crinkle. It is adorable. "What do you mean?" she asks.

"You know, like . . . can we continue . . . this?" I make a vague circular motion.

"Do you mean, like, date? Or just keep . . . talking?"

Huh. That's a good question. I've never dated anyone. If Colby and I date seriously, then I'd have to tell Drew. I'd have to actually *talk* to Drew about what happened between us. At least if I want our friendship to survive, which I do. The idea is probably the worst one I've ever had in my entire life, but I bet Alexis would disagree. Still, I do like the idea of dating Colby. I like the fact that she might like that idea too.

"I'd have to tell Drew," I blurt out.

She frowns before readjusting her mask over her face. "Who?"

I can barely keep the shame from burning my face. How have I not talked about Drew to her? At all? "My best friend," I say. "We've known each other forever. He's gay." I don't know why I add the last part. Especially because I know it's not true. He isn't gay, he's bisexual. I helped him figure that out.

"Okay," Colby says slowly. "Do you, like, need his permission?"

"No, not permission. I mean, it'd be weird for him not to know." Because he should be let down, officially, and not through the grapevine.

"So, after you talk to Drew, your gay best friend, you'll know whether we can date?"

Well, when she puts it like that, it sounds ridiculous.

Her expression confirms as much. "Kind of," I say. I wish I could just say the truth, which is that Drew and I kissed less than two weeks before Colby and I met, and we should have a good, rational conversation about it before I officially move on, but I've been scared to and plus, lately, he's been acting like he's the regional leader of the Black Lives Matter movement, so our ability to communicate has been limited.

Colby whistles to Grim and leads him through a series of puppy push-ups: up, down, up, down. She's distracting herself, and I let her.

"So, my graduation is in a few days," she says, once Grim has finished circling her twice, and then giving two good paw-shakes. "It's gonna be online."

"Oh. Are you sad about that?"

She shrugs. "I was expecting it. I mean, I *was* hoping to walk with my class, you know. Do the whole grand celebration. But they've been telling us for weeks that this is coming. They just confirmed it this morning. Do you know if your school is doing virtual?"

I don't. I actually haven't bothered checking my school mail since I came to San Diego four days ago. "Last I heard, they were still doing in person."

"Is that safe?"

Ha. "I don't know," I say.

"Are you going to go if it's in person?"

"I haven't thought about it."

"Really?" She looks at me in surprise. "But . . . it's graduation. Aren't you excited?"

"You're really the only thing in the last few months that's made me excited." I say it before I process what I've said, and now both my cheeks and ears are on fire. "I mean. Just that, I've been kind of . . . uh."

But for the first time since this conversation started, Colby looks like she's smiling beneath her mask. "Really?"

Good. It looks like I've said at least one completely honest and uncomplicated thing this whole conversation. "Yeah," I say. "Absolutely."

Colby rolls her eyes like she's pushing away the clouds of doubt I'd been summoning like a total jerk. Poirot comes over to lie between us and paws at the ground in front him. He's trying to get Grim to play. Grim noses the ground, whines, and Colby gives him his release signal. "Okay," she says as the two begin to wrestle, like a gentle giant with a tiny ball of yarn. "Well, *I'm* excited about graduation. But also, you know, you're not bad either." She laughs. "At all. So, okay. Fine. Talk to your best friend. But tell me soon, okay? Don't leave me hanging."

"I won't," I say. "I promise."

INTERLUDE #4

IT CAN BE WEIRD TO BE THE YOUNGEST OF two sisters so much older than you. It's like you're in a built-in trio but also totally apart. There are references I don't understand, experiences I haven't shared. Things about the world of dating and jobs and taxes that go totally over my head.

It can be lonely.

I guess that's part of what makes Drew so special to me. We got to grow up together, at least from middle school until now. We became friends because of sixth-grade English, when the teacher insisted I read my essay out loud. We all had to read aloud, it turned out, but I didn't know that when I wrote it. I'd written it about how Harry Styles from One Direction was an excellent frontman, but I personally felt that Luke

Hemmings from 5 Seconds of Summer had a better aesthetic.

I was twelve and it was a vocabulary exercise. One I thought was just going to be between me and the teacher. So, when Mr. Ranier stood in front of me, arms crossed, lips pursed, and repeating, for the third time, that "The class is waiting," I felt like I was going to melt into a puddle of sweat and terror.

And then Drew faked a heart attack.

I mean, he literally threw himself on the ground, hands pressed to his chest, tongue out, convulsing. I think he thought heart attacks and seizures were the same thing, I don't know. But it worked. Mr. Ranier ran to him, and then as Drew sat back up, panting and coughing, and insisting that he'd live, probably, Mr. Ranier told the rest of us to work quietly while he escorted Drew to the nurse's office.

The next day, at lunch, I asked Drew if he was okay. We were standing in line for stale pizza with a side of peas. He laughed. "I'm fine," he said. "I just thought you were gonna pee your pants."

"You did that for me?"

"Mr. Ranier is a bully sometimes. He doesn't really like hearing *no*. I mean, I know he's the teacher, but it was obvious you were uncomfortable. So, I tried to help."

"That's . . . so cool. Thanks."

He nodded with a cheery smile, pleased and proud. Then, as I followed him to his table, his expression turned thoughtful. "What'd you think of the performance, though? Too much?"

We sat. "Depends on what you were going for. It was believable enough to distract our teacher."

"But how did it make you feel?"

"Uh . . . surprised? Scared?"

He took a bite of his pizza and nodded as he chewed. "Good, good. I can work with that."

"Do you wanna be an actor?"

"Maybe. It's a possibility." His knee bounced. "I'm weighing my options. My mom says I like to talk and be heard. She thinks I should be a lawyer." He took another bite. "But I don't like arguing. Do you?"

"Not really. Or else I guess you wouldn't have had to fake a heart attack yesterday."

He nods. "Makes sense. I like to sing—and dance. Oh! Have you heard about the *Into the Woods* auditions?"

I didn't know there were auditions in the woods. Actually, until that moment, I hadn't ever paid attention to what happened in the school's theater department, or any theater department, ever. My last school performance had been in the third grade, when we learned how to sing the dreidel song, and then I tripped on my dress and face-planted in front of everyone I knew.

But I listened to Drew sing Steven Sondheim's praises, and within days of spending time together at lunch, I learned that *Into the Woods* was a musical, not a location. Then I learned about *West Side Story* and *Sweeney Todd*. I cried when I heard "Think of Me" from *Phantom of the Opera*. I put "Defying Gravity" from *Wicked* on repeat. I fell in love with music and performance, and with Drew. The way friends do.

One day, we sat on the couch watching Renée Elise Goldsberry's Mimi sing about her impending death in *Rent*. Then Drew sat up suddenly and said, "That's what I want."

"To . . . die from drug addiction and HIV?"

"No—"

"Get ignored by a cruel government on top of being unable to pay rent?"

"No—hush, man." I dodged the throw pillow he tossed in my direction, but he was smiling. "I want my voice to matter, to make change. You know Jonathan Larson wasn't even gay? Here's this white, straight, cisgender Jewish guy free of disease and he creates this . . . this masterpiece, about love, and joy, and people telling the system to eff off. I want to do that."

I was about to make another joke to clarify whether he was specifically saying he wanted to tell the system to "eff off" (neither of us felt comfortable actually cursing until sometime in the last two years), but then I looked at him. At his fresh fade and the curls atop his head, the way his clean white sneakers tapped against the carpet, how he was leaning forward, eyes laser-focused as he planted his chin on folded hands. He was serious. *This* was serious.

"What about you?" he asked, turning his head slightly to train his light brown eyes on me.

I looked at the screen, which had moved on to the characters Roger and Mark yelling at each other, and then back at him. They were singing about their friendship and their fears about being abandoned. "I just want to be here," I said. It wasn't the most revolutionary statement, but it was how I felt. How I still feel, I guess.

People always have their big dreams, their grand plans. Their hopes to change the world or speak truth to power or, I don't know, *have* power. Use it or abuse it or what have you. And me? I just want to enjoy the ride. I just want to enjoy being alive. Can't that be enough?

Drew didn't seem disappointed by my answer. Not then anyway. He just nodded, like what I said made perfect sense, and then leaned back, still thoughtful, still totally enamored with the performance, and the message, that lay before us. "That's cool," he said. "I want to be here too." He grinned at me. "With you, at least."

At the time, well . . . that certainly did seem like enough, for both of us. But I guess you can't stay twelve forever.

CHAPTER SIXTEEN

I HOLD ON TO THE LIGHT FLUTTERY FEELING Colby always leaves me with as Poirot and I walk back to Alexis's house. As soon as we're inside, Poirot runs through Alexis's open bedroom door, and I can see that she's busy packing for our trip home this evening. I sit on the couch and take the opportunity to open my computer. I still don't really want to check my email, but Colby has inspired me, so I scroll for a second, and there, buried amid updates from Broadway.com and a few of my favorite clothing stores, is a big, bold message from the school: GRADUATION UPDATE FOR THE SENIOR CLASS OF 2020.

With a resigned sigh, I click open the email.

It is with deep sadness and regret that we inform our Irvine City High School students that this year's graduation will be virtual . . .

I tell myself I don't care. That online or in person, I wasn't looking forward to it anyway. The same way I wasn't looking forward to prom, which was canceled, or the variety show Drew had been planning as part of his senior project, which was also canceled. He never talks about it anyway. For a brief, bitter moment, I tell myself that's why he's so eager to plan all these protests—an opportunity to still be the star of something. Then I feel so miserably guilty that I'm tempted to just throw my computer onto the ground, maybe stomp on it for good measure. It's only the realization that Poirot has stumbled back into the living room and is now gently pushing his nose against my knees that stops me. Calms me and keeps me present.

Well then. I guess that's that. So, I'm not gonna see Size D Rebecca in person or sit next to Drew making silly faces while Brae-Lynn, the valedictorian, takes civil rights quotes out of context and applies them to our journey as citizens of the world. So, I'm not gonna celebrate with the people I've known for almost half my life or wear the obligatory black cap and gown that looks sort of silly but is still meant to represent that we're now adults, ready—or mostly ready—for the real world. So, I'm gonna miss out on the one life ceremony every single high school student in this country is supposed to have. So what. It's just one more thing this hellish year is taking away from me.

Selfishly, I send Drew a new text message (**Did you see the school email?**), but he doesn't respond. He hasn't responded to any of the texts I've sent since this morning. I'm almost tempted to call his mom, just to be extra, but instead I close my laptop and pick up Poirot, who's now gnawing on the toes of my socks. I lean back on the couch and pull him up to my chest. His soft, furry body is soothing and warm. A little life, so small and yet so free, full of the simplest sort of wonder. You wouldn't think such a thing could bring so much comfort and yet . . .

"You good?" Alexis says from her door. She looks at me and I brush away the tears that have sprung to the corners of my eyes.

"Yup," I say. Alexis cocks her head at me, but I give her a wobbly smile and let Poirot, who started wiggling as soon as he saw her, back onto the ground.

"I'm going to grab a coffee before we go," Alexis says. "My last pre-extreme-quarantine treat. Do you want to come with me?"

I shake my head, not because coffee is unappetizing but because, somehow, leaving her apartment has suddenly become the very last thing I want to do. I watch quietly as she dresses Poirot again, slips on her puppy go bag, and heads back out the door. In their absence, I look around her apartment—the two windows across from the pullout sofa I'm sitting on, which let in streams of light that Poirot loves to play in; the little kitchen nook where we discovered Alexis was out of food, and then again, where she admonished me for wanting to go to a silly high school party. And it *was* silly; I know that now. And yet, it was the last real high school thing I'll ever get to do. I had thought, before I came here, that my final chances for a real senior year experience were over, and then I met Colby. Colby, the first real-life person I've had a real-life crush on. Colby, the first girl I've ever kissed. And now I'm angry, because Mel chose a terrible time to wake up, and now I'm angrier, because what the hell kind of thought is that? What the hell kind of sister am I?

The tears fall faster than I can stop them, so I don't try to. Instead, I let them stream down my cheeks. No, I don't let them. I force them. I heave hard, ragged, and ruthless, like a punishment—or a prayer, I can't begin to tell. I curl into myself, bring my fingers to my hair, gripping into pain, into release, into nothingness.

And then there's nothing left to give. It's just me and my breath, fast and shallow, until it's not. I wipe my eyes, and the friction hurts like hell. I stand and walk slowly to Alexis's bathroom and turn on the cold water, running my fingers beneath it and pressing them to the corners of my stinging eyes. When I hear the front door open, I flush the toilet—hold five seconds, as usual, so that Alexis doesn't suspect anything. And yet, when I see her, I do the only thing that makes sense: I wrap my arms around her waist, and I don't let go. If she's surprised, she doesn't show it. Instead, she holds me tight. She doesn't let go either.

Later, after Alexis is ready, I've taken out the trash, and we've packed up the car, we give our attention, again, to Poirot. Alexis spends a lot of time hugging him, and I don't blame her. His puppy dog eyes are big, and his long tail is so low that it's nearly tucked beneath him. I lean down after Alexis finally lets go and give him a quick rub between the ears. His tail wags a bit at that, and my heart tugs. I scoop him up one last time because, yes, I am going to miss him. A lot.

"I'll come visit again," I whisper into one of his floppy ears. He licks my face, and I say *yuck* to preserve my reputation, but it takes far too much strength to put him back down and walk away.

In the car, I try to let my eyes and body finally rest, but a voice from the radio blares on again. "In yet another update from Councilman Lowry, a new measure has been introduced to implement a curfew, discouraging Black Lives Matter protesters . . ."

"Sorry," Alexis mutters. "Sorry, sorry." The radio voice disappears, and Alexis skips through the tracks of her music library, before landing on "Home" from *The Wiz*. She's trying to make me feel better, but it only reminds me of Drew. She might as well have kept the radio on. Still, I decide to try texting him one last time. Just in case.

On the way home, I write.

To my relief, he responds. It's a thumbs-up emoji.

Alexis looks over at my phone screen. "Well," she says. "At least that's something."

CHAPTER SEVENTEEN

TWO HOURS LATER, MOM AND DAD GREET us at the door, hugging us with smiles and laughter, as if we'd just returned home from a war well-won. It's no slobbery, tail-wagging puppy greeting, but it's nice. Honestly, it's more than nice. It's amazing; Dad's eyes are bright and alive, and Mom looks like she's actually slept for the first time in her life. The smiles on my parent's faces are genuine, with no ticking time bombs beneath them. Mel's not here, but she could be, she *will* be, and all of us, finally, *finally*, can breathe.

Alexis drops her bags off in her old bedroom, and I retreat to mine. At first, I sit on my bed, and then I lie on it, sinking into the feeling of a cushion that is *not* a series of metal springs covered by the promise of thread.

Oh, how I missed this bed. In fact, I missed my whole room, in part because my privacy will no longer be defiled by the opening of the front door. It's not big, by any means, certainly smaller than a living room, even of a one-bedroom apartment. But I've got a few posters on my wall—mostly playbills of my favorite musicals—and a bookshelf of my favorite manga and knickknacks, like a Pop! figurine of Renée Elise Goldberry's Angelica Schuyler.

On the back of my closed door is the huge poster of Amber Liu, her tanned abs peeking out from beneath an oversize white tee. And across from the side of my bed is one huge window that overlooks the street outside, which is perfect for anyone wanting to reenact that famous scene from *Say Anything* where the boy stands outside the window of his paramour with a radio held above his head as he professes his love. Drew proved this by doing just that, two Valentine's Days ago, as a random precursor to a movie marathon we had in lieu of dates, because we have both always been chronically single. Until now, I guess.

I wait a few beats to let that sink in. Then I reach for my phone. There's a text message from Colby already waiting.

Did you get home safe?

It's only from a few minutes ago. I respond **yes** quickly and then, **I miss you already.**

Really?

Yeah. Definitely.

So, I'm really going to see you again?

To answer her, I start a video call.

"Hello?"

I grin. "Hi. See? You're seeing me again."

"Wow." She rolls her eyes playfully. "Well, I guess that's a good sign."

"It is," I say. "Promise."

"Is it nice to be home?"

"Yeah," I say. I lie back on the bed with an arm folded beneath my head. "My parents are really, really happy. I'm happy to see them too."

"That's good," she says. "Will you get to see Mel soon?"

I sigh. "Not yet. She'll be out of the hospital tonight or tomorrow, I think, and then we'll have to figure out all the quarantine, social-distancing, blah blah blah stuff. Not, like, blah blah blah, in a bad way. Just. It's a lot of planning, just to spend time with someone."

"I know," she says. "But it's good, yeah? That you're taking all the precautions. It's good you're taking care of each other." For a moment, her voice gets quiet, and I'm reminded of her uncle. The one who died from Covid. I remember to be extra cautious when I talk about seeing Mel. Extra grateful too.

"How's your mom?" I ask.

She smiles at me, like she's surprised I remembered. "She's doing her best, I guess. We're down a pack of toilet paper and she hasn't started to panic yet. So, that's progress."

"It is," I agree. "Speaking of pandemic prepping, guess what?"

"Hmm?"

"Turns out we're doing virtual graduation, too, after all. Yaaaay."

"I'm sorry," she says.

"It's fine."

"Really?"

"No." I laugh. "I'm actually super bummed about it. But I guess I'm just getting used to being bummed."

"Because this year continues to be mind-numbingly bad?"

"Something like that. But you know what I'm grateful for?"

"Hmm?"

"You." Her phone shifts and suddenly all I can see is her popcorn ceiling. Then the video adjusts, and I see her eyes peeking out from behind her arms. "I'm serious." I laugh. "Because of you, this year doesn't feel like a total wash. It feels . . . I don't know. Exciting. But also, warm, and stable too. I guess. I don't know." Now it's my turn to feel shy and embarrassed. I scrunch up my nose and cover my face with my hand.

"I know what you mean," she whispers softly. "I feel that way too."

"Yeah?"

She smiles, moving her own arms to reveal the softness in her eyes. "Yeah."

"Cool," I say. Because it is. Super cool.

We end up talking for another hour before I hear a gentle knock on my door. It's my mom. She pokes her head in to let me know it's time for dinner.

"I'll talk to you tomorrow?" I ask Colby.

"Yes, please," she says, and I hang up just as Mom quirks her head at me quizzically.

"Who's that?" she asks.

"Oh." I blanch. I have not talked to my parents about liking girls yet. I don't even know where I'd begin. Maybe my first day back from San Diego on the first day that my sister has awakened from a coma isn't the time to try it. "Just a friend," I say. "I met her at the dog park."

Mom raises an eyebrow. "Okay." She takes a step

into my room and looks around. I guess she probably doesn't come in here very often. I wonder what she sees when she looks at it. What it reveals about me to her. "I got the email from your school, by the way. About graduation."

"Oh." I'm even more reluctant to talk about that.

"Do you want to—"

"I'm okay," I say. She peers at me closely, and for a flash, I'm reminded of the last few days before I left for San Diego, when Dad would try to watch me surreptitiously, checking for any cracks beneath the facade, any signs he missed with Mel that he wanted to be sure he caught with me. I sigh deeply. "Really," I say. "I'm fine."

"Okay," she says. "But it's okay to be upset about it too. I would be."

I consider that. I genuinely don't want to talk about it, but it does help, I guess. Knowing that she'd be upset too. Knowing that it's not a silly thing to be upset over. "Even with everything else going on?" I ask. "You'd be upset about graduation?"

"Oh honey," Mom says. "Yes. There's no . . . hierarchy of pain, here. Graduation is a big deal, and you don't get to experience it the way everyone else usually does. That sucks."

Oh God, I'm gonna cry again. "Thanks, Mom," I say. I breathe out. "I'll be down in a second."

She smiles at me and then turns to face the door. She pauses at the image of Amber Liu. It's literally the only image I have on my walls that is not an ode to show tunes. She chuckles softly and turns back toward me. "Tell your new friend I said hi," she says with a wink, before continuing through the door and closing it softly behind her.

After dinner, I head back up to my room and slip into bed. I'm ready to call it a night, but I want to read the email from the school again. I don't know why. I guess to remind myself that it's real or vaccinate myself against the gnawing disappointment. But when I open my email, another message greets me.

The subject is blank, but it's from Mel.

I read it, and then I read it again, and again, and again. And I let myself fall asleep, tears soft but welcome, eternally grateful that this isn't the last message from my big sister that I'll ever read.

EMAIL FROM MEL

Hey, sis,

Thanks for texting me over the last few days. I have a lot to catch up on. A lot of texts, actually, and a bunch of other stuff. Emailing feels a little less overwhelming than using my phone right now. But I wanted to say that I love you, and I'm sorry I scared you. I wish I could give a good explanation, but I don't know that there is one. Sometimes, things just feel hopeless, you know? But reading your texts when I got home tonight was nice. Like I didn't miss too much. But like there's a lot I could've. So, for that, I don't know. I'm grateful.

Listen, about Drew: He will understand. He loves you, and he's your boy. Heartbreak is never easy, no matter how old we get, but a strong friendship will weather the toughest storms. Plus, you're both theater geeks—you understand big, complicated feelings! Just talk to him, be kind, be open, and remember to treat each other with love.

And Colby!!!! Okay, that's exciting!!! She's cute, she's smart, she's kind, she trains dogs—but don't tell me you've gone over to the dark side now? Are you a DOG lover? What's going on there? Looks like Colby's got some superpowers. I'm glad you met her. She sounds like a keeper. Have you told Mom and Dad yet? If not, don't trip. Between you and me, they kind of . . . suspected. But don't tell them I told you that.

Anyway, I hope everything's good with you, still. I understand what it's like to feel like you're failing people. Trust me. And maybe I'm not the best person to give advice, because I know . . . I know how easy it is to feel tired. To give up. But listen, living isn't about being right, okay? Or being perfect. It's just about being you. That's the only thing anyone can ask from you. And no matter what, your family loves you. Drew loves you. Apparently, Poirot loves you. And guess what? A cute girl you just met thinks you're pretty cool too.

I'd call that the opposite of failing, little sis.

Anyway, okay, my eyes are drooping. That's enough screen time for me.

I love you, always.

Love, your big sister,
Mel

CHAPTER EIGHTEEN

THE NEXT DAY, I SEND MEL A GOOD MORNING text. I want to text her more; tell her all the little things swirling in my head as always, but now that she's awake, it feels different. For one thing, she probably needs more time to take care of herself; for another, I know I can text her now and she'll actually respond. There's not a desperate need to keep her up to date, because I know I'll get to tell her in person eventually. Still, when I get a text back a minute later ('Sup), it stirs my heart. Reminds me that a seemingly shattered world doesn't always lose all its pieces.

I rub my eyes and fix my hair. Then I snap a few smiling photos of myself to send to Colby. She responds with her own cute photo, positioned beneath the camera, smiling above Grim as he shoves his head in a bowl of food.

What are those images above your bed? she texts.

I look up, like I've almost forgotten them myself. They're mostly fan art printouts of various anime characters stuck on my wall like a collage, plus a string of photos of Drew and me over the years. The pictures that Colby can see best, based on the selfies I sent her, are from last year's performance of *Seussical*. Drew played Horton the Elephant, and I was in the audience, cheering him on. We took a pic backstage after, me in long boho braids and a maroon Irvine City High School sweatshirt, and him in a gray bowl hat outfitted with huge gray elephant ears. We're holding each other tightly and grinning like mad.

Some anime fan art and me and my bestie.

How long have you known each other?

Since middle school. Sixth grade. He introduced me to musicals.

Ah, so he's the culprit.

He'll gladly take the blame. Trust me.

Suddenly, my phone buzzes, because now Colby is calling. "Hi," she says when I answer. "Grim and I are going on a walk so I thought I'd just call, if that's okay?"

"Of course. Yes. Hi!" I scoot to the end of my bed so

my feet touch the floor, and I slouch forward, pressing the phone closer to my ear. "How are you?"

"I'm good," she says, her voice slightly out of breath. I imagine Grim walking quickly, taking huge sniffs of bushes and grass while his regal tail is proudly lifted in the air. "So, I was curious. Are musicals what you're gonna study in college?" Colby asks.

"At Chapman?" I shrug. "I don't know. I thought I'd take some courses, maybe."

"Will you write music—or perform?"

"No." I laugh. "My dad is the musician, remember? And my mom and Alexis sing a little, but . . . that bug kind of missed me."

"Do you like to write?"

I frown, considering the question. "I don't *not* like to write." I've always gotten straight As in English anyway.

"You could be a culture critic," she says. "My dad is a journalist for the *San Diego Tribune*. Mostly, he covers local news and events. But he's always talking about their music guy and their museum guy and whatever. They're not staff writers, but they send articles to him to review."

"Oh wow. I didn't know your dad was a journalist."

She giggles. "Yeah. My mom is a graphic designer. That's how they met, a hundred years ago."

"So, do you think you'll do something like that, too? From your boat on the ocean?"

"No." She heaves a heavy sigh. "Probably not. My dad's been really stressed out with the pandemic happening, and then the protests, and my mom keeps having to put together all these, like . . . infographics or whatever about rising death rates. With my uncle passing, too, it's like they can't escape the absolute worst of reality, every day, even if they get paid for it."

I can't even imagine how awful that would be. "I'm sorry," I say. "Guess living on a boat seems like a good way to take a break."

I hear her shift on the phone and then snap out a quick and firm command to Grim. "Sorry," she says. "He saw a dog he didn't like and started to get grumpy. Anyway, yeah, yes. That's why I want to try out ocean living, for a while. Just rocking out on the sea for a bit and not having to worry about doing a job that stresses me out so that I can keep paying rent, or a mortgage, or whatever. I mean, I don't want to do it forever. In college, I think I want to study . . ." She pauses, and for a second, I think she's distracted by Grim again, but when the pause goes on for too long, I prompt her.

"What?" I ask. Then I think about what I know already—how the first time I saw her, I thought she went to a fancy, private high school, because of how neat and proper she looked; how the next time I saw her, she was in a flirty, fashionable dress. How every time I see her, she looks gorgeous, and not just because I have a very obvious crush on her. “Let me guess—is it fashion?”

At that, she lets out a surprised laugh. “Maybe. Good guess.”

“I’m getting to know you,” I say with a smug smile that I’m sure she can hear in my voice.

“Good,” she says. “I’m glad you want to.”

My smile is permanent; it will never leave my face again. “Me too,” I say. Then, because it’s on my mind, I add, “It’s kind of wild that I’m just learning these little things about you, though, or about your parents, anyway, when I feel like we’ve had these big milestones already, like kissing and . . . and . . .”

“Trauma bonding?” she asks. It’s an amused tone, but I can feel the undercurrent of it—the sadness.

“Yeah,” I say softly. “Like, first we met when I thought Poirot was done for; then I met you again at Paw House, where that lady was being awful; then, later, we kissed and immediately after we were verbally attacked by some dude, and . . . then my sister woke up from a coma, and I’m here.”

“It *is* a lot,” Colby agrees. “But I thought you were cute the moment I saw you. And I’ve really liked talking to you since . . .”

Suddenly my lips are dry. "Yeah, me too." It comes out as a whisper. "I saw you and thought, *Wow*. And if I have to deal with an angry white guy in a bar just to keep holding your hand, then I will." She lets out a breathless laugh, but I'm serious. This is what it is, right? To be who we are, look how we do, *love* as we do, and live in this world? These are the cards we've been dealt. So, screw it. I'll play to win. "When's your virtual graduation?"

"Hmm? Oh." She clears her throat. "Uh, it's tomorrow, actually. Why?"

"Can I watch it?"

At this, she lets out a loud guffaw. "Seriously?"

"Yeah," I say brightly. "Send me the link. Let's add to the beautiful and traumatic life experiences we've already had together."

"Is graduation beautiful and traumatic?"

"Isn't it?"

"Touché." She laughs again, and I vow that my mission, for as long as Colby will let me, is to make her laugh like that every single day. "Okay, sure," she says. "I'll send you mine if you send me yours."

So, there it is. Our first official date, kind of. We agree to watch each other's ceremonies, and I promise to be extra attentive: I will text about every ridiculous yearbook photo, bad speech, amazing hairdo, and more. I don't know why, but it excites me. Finally, graduation feels like something to look forward to. Finally, I feel like there are pieces of my life that I can control. They might be little. Barely tangible, even, but at least I know they exist.

CHAPTER NINETEEN

WHEN COLBY AND I FINALLY HANG UP AN hour later, it's only because Alexis tells me to *Get off the phone with my girlfriend*, and I holler at her to *Shut up, please.* Then I emerge from my room to see her waiting outside. She waggles her eyebrows at me as I pass, and I give her the middle finger. To retaliate, she follows me with a high, squeaky voice: "'You hang up! No, *you* hang up!'" she crows. She only stops when we reach the top of the steps, probably because our parents could hear. Then she sticks her tongue out at me, nudges me aside, and races to the bottom of the steps first.

Ugh. Sisters.

In the living room, Mom is tucked beneath Dad's arm as they cuddle up on the sofa, watching another episode of the rebooted *Twilight Zone* series. Alexis plops on the couch beside them, her phone already in her hand, looking more like a disaffected teenager than a corporate project manager in her early thirties. It's an image I want to hold in my mind forever, because here is my family: happy, and healthy, and whole. And with our parents home and Mel out of the hospital, Alexis gets to just be another daughter in the house, instead of a surrogate mother hen. Which means that when she puts her phone to her ear because, "Oh! Houston is calling," I can't help but rag on her the way she did to me earlier.

"'Oh, my husband is calling,'" I whine in a high-pitched voice. "'Everyone, be quiet!'"

This time, she sticks her middle finger up at me, and then my mother gives us both The Glare. Okay, got it. Not in front of the parents.

Still, I amuse myself by making silly faces at her while she asks Houston about his trip to LA and then asks more about the fact that Parakeet Man apparently left another series of flyers around the neighborhood this morning, this time about the tyranny of curfews.

"I can't believe I agree with him," Alexis mutters.

I can't hear Houston's response, but then she says, "Ha, I know. What if his next flyer is about how Black lives matter?"

No one is talking to me, but I take it upon myself

to jokingly add, "I mean, people contain multitudes." My English teacher would be proud—that's a Walt Whitman quote I learned last year.

"Tia says people contain multitudes," Alexis informs Houston, and I hear the deep rumble of his laughter. She listens for a beat and then gives me a sly look.

"Houston wants to know if you want him to send you pics of Poirot."

Ugh, I hate the spark of excitement that just shot through me. Yes! The answer, obviously, is yes. Who am I? What have I become? "Sure," I say nonchalantly, but when my phone buzzes and a series of increasingly ridiculous images of Poirot come through, I feel my face morph into that hideous cooing expression I've seen on Alexis's face too many times before. I can't hide it; it's too late.

"What are you looking at?" Mom asks.

"Poirot," I coo—apparently I'm a cooer now—and Mom sticks her hand out.

"Let me see!"

And so then, there we are; my parents and me, cooing together over my sister's smush-faced mutt while Alexis takes the opportunity to escape to another room for privacy. When we're done looking at the photos, Mom hands my phone back to me and then raises her hand with an "Oh!" as if she just remembered something.

"Tia, by the way, why did Drew text me for Mel's address this morning?"

I blink at her. "What?"

"Drew. He texted me, asking for Mel's address. Why didn't he just ask you?"

The warm gooey feeling I've been having all morning calcifies in my stomach. "I don't know," I say, although I do know, and I'm not planning on telling her why. "I'll be right back." Then I hustle up to my room, where I clench and unclench my fist while Amber Liu stares at me accusingly from the closed door. I text Drew.

> Seriously? You can text my MOM, but you can't text me?

I wait a minute, then five, then ten. He doesn't respond.

Finally, I rummage through my closet for a jacket, grab a stray mask from my dresser, and stomp back down the stairs, shouting "I'll be right back!" before I close the front door behind me. I don't have a plan of where I'm going, but we have a neighborhood park just past the community pool and tennis court, and it's a nice day: warm and sunny, and basically devoid of people.

I walk down the winding, tree-lined path toward the

park. It's kind of eerie . . . realizing that I'm home now, a comfortable place I've known all my life, that's quiet and lovely and yet suddenly so . . . isolated. I can hear the birds; the wind rustling through the trees; the distant buzz of someone's lawn mower somewhere I can't see. I take my eyes off my feet and look up, in case I might catch a neighbor or two.

After a few minutes of walking, I see a white man and his two kids sitting outside their open garage. He's working on his car, and the kids are drawing with chalk on the driveway pavement. Unlike my usual self, I smile and wave. He waves back, offers a perfectly nice "Good morning," and that should feel at least somewhat sufficient. But then I see the flag above his front door, with the words *Blue Lives Matter* waving proudly in the clear, cloudless sky.

Maybe he thinks it's a harmless message of solidarity for the "boys in blue," the good apples, not the bad. Maybe he doesn't understand that he's negating a simple message, which is that, yes, everyone's lives matter, but most people think ours—including mine, a Black girl's—don't. Shouldn't. I could say something to him. I even *want* to, and that—that instinct—terrifies me. Because what would I say? And worse, much worse, how would he respond?

I think back to the night on the boardwalk: to the man who acted like an ally only to attempt assault and hurl abuse when he didn't get what he wanted. I think about our teacher, trying to start a discussion on rhetoric and ending class because students wanted to talk about how guns were more important than people. I think about Robbie, sweet, straight A Robbie, who I still haven't texted, who says things like "doggone," and "crud," who was arrested because he threw a balled-up piece of paper that the police thought was a weapon. I think I'm thinking too much, when all I wanted to do was go for a walk. Clear my mind.

So, I put my head down and keep walking.

A few long minutes later, I'm at the neighborhood park. It's small, in comparison to the city park in North Hills, but clean and quaint as ever. A mom is having a picnic with her toddler; two preteens are hitting a volleyball over a net with atrociously bad form; a man is looking at his phone while his Chihuahua sniffs the bushes. They are all white, every single person. And so what? This is my neighborhood—it has been, my whole life. And yet, suddenly, I feel unsafe. Exposed. Maybe, if I'm even the tiniest bit honest with myself, that's what makes me hate these protests so much. That even if I'm quiet, other people are making me stand out . . . and then what?

I pull my jacket tighter around me and walk to an empty swing. There, swaying with the push and pull of my feet and legs, I bring up the *OC Register*.

Irvine City High School Student Arrested at School Protest

On Sunday, May 31, 2020, Irvine City High School student Robert "Robbie" Wakefield was arrested on suspicion of assault with a deadly weapon while attending an unsanctioned protest regarding accusations of racism and poor classroom management that occurred in an online class earlier this week.

Andrew "Drew" Moore, one of the students responsible for organizing the protest, claims that Robert threw a wadded-up piece of paper, though police claim the evidence is inconclusive. ICHS parent Ramona Baker, who attended a counterprotest with parents, noted that the message of Black Lives Matter, a group she claims promotes local terrorism, is indoctrinating students online. "This is why I encourage the school board to reconsider online classes and return to in-person education as soon as possible," Baker says.

I try not to claw my eyes out as I scan the rest of the article. At least it looks like Drew and Robbie's mom pulled bail, like Drew said they would. Good. That's good. I click out of the article, put my phone away. Then I pull out my phone again and send two messages: the first to Robbie, to tell him I hope he's okay, and the next to Drew.

The night Colby and I went out, a guy, a white guy, tried to kiss us—one of us, both of us. I don't know, whatever he could get. When we tried to get away, he told us that's why we keep getting killed. He meant Black people.

At first, I don't think Drew is going to respond, still. And maybe he shouldn't. I don't know what I want him to say anyway. But then—

Jesus. Are you okay?

Yes. Technically. You know?

Yeah. I do.

[. . .]

I love you.

I love you too.

He doesn't say anything else, and neither do I. I just sit in the park, letting the hinges of the swing creak back and forth, and telling myself that one day, hopefully soon, all this, everything we're going through, will be a thing of the distant past.

INTERLUDE #5

YOU KNOW HOW SOMETIMES YOU REMEMber that your parents lived through historical events? Like, to you, it's something you read about in your textbook, in history or social studies or something, and then you do the math, and you're like, oh wait, my parents were alive in the 1960s. You remember that the past was once someone's present. If not your parents, then someone close to them. Maybe a cousin, or an uncle, or a grandparent. Or their parent.

You remember that stories often contain some piece of truth, and whatever feels distant was once, for someone, frighteningly, devastatingly close.

Mom was born the year after Emmett Till was killed; Dad was born the year after that. Dad was six and Mom was seven when Dr. Martin Luther King Jr.

gave his *I Have a Dream* speech. They were seven and nine respectively when Malcolm X was shot.

I know this because I mapped their ages for a class project in middle school.

You think, sometimes, that history is a thing that happens to other people. And that when it happens, it happens outside the flow of time. It doesn't occur to you that your mom, like my mom, might have been celebrating her birthday when Malcolm X was shot. Her family—our family—learned about it that day on the news. Mom has said that all she remembers is cake and tears.

Sometimes, when you think about the amount of devastation and turmoil and heartbreak that occurs alongside birthdays and anniversaries and falling in love and going to school—well, sometimes you wonder how anyone is able to keep it together. Keep going, and pretend you're not bursting at the seams, ready to let everything fall apart, like stars scattered across the sky, bright and dying before you even knew they existed.

CHAPTER TWENTY

FOR SOME REASON, COLBY'S GRADUATION is at nine in the morning on Friday, even though it's online. Why our schools insist on our suffering, I don't know, but at least Colby looks stunning. She hasn't appeared on-screen yet, but she sent me two photos this morning, with her hair freshly cropped with the help of her dad, and her eyes lined in a bright purple, with a gentle pink gloss applied to her lips.

The first picture is a selfie of her alone: In it, she's wearing huge gold earrings, black jeans with carefully applied rips at the knees paired with a crisp green button-down, and a black tie with faint floral patterns in gray. In the second image, she's sandwiched between her dad, a man about her height with lighter brown skin and short, thick hair, and her mom, a woman with slightly more melanin and long Senegalese twists. Colby's eyes are closed, but her mouth is wide and toothy, showing off that loveable front gap, while both parents grin with obvious pride. Their joy makes me hopeful, reminds me that these silly life events are eventful for a reason: They give us a chance to remind each other that we are loved. And I am happy seeing that even in this uncertain world, the love in Colby's life is so clearly abundant.

An hour passes while I sit at the dining table in the room adjacent to the kitchen, texting Colby as promised while we both watch the speeches from her principal and vice principal, and various students, including one who clearly dreams of being cast on *Saturday Night Live* one day. I bet ze will include it in zir audition reel. Honestly, I'm not even mad—I chuckled once or twice.

Finally, the graduating students' names are read aloud, and as they are, their yearbook photo pops up, with present students typing their acknowledgments in the chat. Highlights include *yezzer*, *got 'em!*, and *wuddup, tho?*

When I hear Colby's name, I sit up straight and pull the computer closer, nearly knocking over the iced tea I've been sipping on. Her yearbook photo comes up a second later, and she looks lovely as always, but I'm surprised to see long Senegalese twists flowing past her shoulders. I desperately grasp around for my phone like it's not right next to my hand.

You look like your mom!

I know! Trust. She loves when people ask if we're sisters.

Is that why you cut your hair? I mean, I know the twists aren't real, but you know what I mean.

No, but I should tell her that. She'll be so mad.

But I just wanted to try something new.

Do you like the long hair better?

I like you.

Good answer!

"Is that the girl you met at the dog park?"

I jump at the sound of my mom's voice behind me, and this time the iced tea does spill. "Holy crap, Mom! What are you, a ninja?"

Mom puts her hands up in apology and then shuffles past me into the kitchen, where there are paper towels on one of the counters. "Soooorry," she says, in a way that means she's probably not that sorry. "And yes. I am a ninja. Thank you for asking." I roll my eyes as I take the paper towel from her hands and wipe my part of the table. "So," she says when I'm done.

I look up. "So what?"

"Is that the girl?"

I blink too many times and probably sputter too. For a second, I'm reminded of the heart attack Drew had in English class all those years ago. Funny, I feel like I'm having one now. "Uh . . ."

Mom's eyes roll up to the ceiling, like she's thinking, and then she looks off to the side. "You know," she begins conversationally. "When Mel came home with her first girlfriend, it was a total shock to me and your dad. Mostly because she'd dated like three different boys in rapid succession right before that." She waves her hand dismissively. "You know your sister. But then she walked in with a girl one day–I don't know, you were probably a baby still, or a toddler–and says, *This is my girlfriend, so-and-so. We're going to go upstairs to study.* And then she walked away, just like that."

God, Mel is too cool sometimes. I can't even imagine. Still, I don't look at my mom. I just push my soggy paper towel to the side and then stare, hard, at Colby's graduation stream, which is coming to an end anyway. But I do manage to say, "And what'd you do?"

Mom shrugs. "I mean," she huffs. "At first, I was

upset. I'm not proud of how I reacted. It was a tense few days. And then Alexis sat me and your dad down and said that if we had a problem with it, we could keep it to ourselves, because what she *wasn't* going to do was let her sister be made to feel ashamed for who she was. And then she instructed us to educate ourselves and sent us half a dozen articles, a couple of books, and the link to a group for parents of queer kids."

"Well. That sounds like Alexis."

"It does." Mom laughs. "And that's when I realized that we raised Alexis to be that way: independent, and brave, and kind. At least I hope that came from us. And I realized we raised Mel to be that way too. It took some time, but eventually, I realized just how brave Mel was, too, to be honest and visible, when it might've been easier to hide."

"Are you still upset, though? Like, cool, she's brave, but do you think you'd be happier if she weren't gay?" I'm still not looking at Mom.

"I'm happy that she's alive," Mom says. When I look up, she's looking at me, her expression serious and laser-focused. "I couldn't care less about anything else. If she's straight, wonderful. If she's gay, wonderful. If she's—what is it? Asexual? That's wonderful too. But if she's happy? Now, *that's* my job to focus on. I brought her into this world, after all. My job is to make sure she thrives in it." Mom takes a deep breath. "Do you understand?"

I duck my head, jiggle the mouse of my laptop so that the darkened screen comes back to life. "Yeah," I mutter.

"Great!" Mom says brightly. She walks over to me and presses a hard, smothery kiss to my cheek, which I know she's doing to annoy me.

"Okay, okay, thanks, Mom."

She winks and then shuffles back through the kitchen, toward the living room, her own laptop somehow magically appearing in her hand, probably so she can do work.

And God, now I want to text Mel again. But since I don't want to be selfish, I consider texting Drew, except he probably doesn't want to hear about Mom catching me watching Colby's graduation, so I lean back in my chair and stare up at the ceiling. Alexis and Dad are both upstairs. I could try talking to one of them. Or Mom again, I guess.

Then I remember what Colby said about her Dad being a journalist, about me writing things. I take a deep breath, open a Word doc on my laptop screen, and start to type. It works like a pressure valve, releasing the tension that's built up over the last few minutes, bleeding out fear and insecurity so that I feel a little lighter, a little more carefree.

Mel calls me five minutes later. I scramble to pick it up.

"Hey!" I say with a smile.

"Yo," she says. "Hey, so I don't know if you want to give me his number or anything, but your boy stopped by earlier. I mean, I didn't see him, but I got, like, two dozen baked brownies and a bunch of flowers dropped off at my door, saying it was from the Moore family. Moore is Drew's last name, right?"

I shake my head, not knowing if what I feel is affection or irritation. "Yeah," I say. "You want to thank him?"

"Yup," Mel says. "It's sweet. Are you guys talking more?"

"Trying to," I say. I give her his number, and then I ask how she's doing.

"Oh, you know," she says. "I mean, taking it day by day. Brownies help."

I laugh. "I bet."

She yawns. "Okay, let me text him and then I'm gonna go. But listen, hey, this is a good sign, right? Him sending your sister something?"

"Well, he's a good guy," I say. "He was worried about you."

Mel sighs. "Yeah." She sighs again and then tells me she loves me.

"I know," I say. "I love you too. You know that, right? How much we all love you?"

Mel coughs, says something I can't hear, and then, "Yeah. I do. Really. Thanks, sis."

"You're welcome," I say, even though I want to tell her that I don't want to be thanked. I don't want anything, except for her to be okay, and to keep being okay. For her to know that she's loved and wanted, no matter how hopeless she might feel sometimes. How alone. Then it clicks, really, what my mom was trying to say.

So, when Mel and I hang up, I go to find Mom again. She's sitting at the counter island that separates the kitchen from the living room, typing on her laptop. I push it away and bury my head in her shoulder. She pauses, probably out of surprise, and then lays her head on my mine, and I soak in the fact that I might be isolated in this house, and sad, and exhausted sometimes, but at least I'm not alone.

CHAPTER TWENTY-ONE

A DAY LATER, I'M STANDING IN FRONT OF MY mirror, wearing my black cap and gown. My parents want to take photos, even if I'm not going to walk. It does feel sort of silly, but as I look at myself, with makeup Alexis did for me, and gold studs I borrowed from her, I'm happy they insisted. I don't get to experience the whole shebang, but at least I get to experience some of it.

"Tia!" My mom shouts from the bottom of the stairs. "Are you ready?"

We literally aren't going anywhere, so I don't know why she's in a rush, but I know better than to let my mom call my name twice. "Yes!" I shout, and then meet her downstairs, where she and Dad and Alexis are standing. Dad has a bouquet of roses he must've ordered from the outside world. He hands them to me as I approach, and then the three of them converge like a wave, passing around hugs and kisses and congratulations.

"Thanks, guys," I whisper. Mom proceeds to act as if she's been possessed by a fashion photographer and directs me into various poses: with the flowers, without the flowers, with the cap, without the cap, next to Alexis, with Dad on the other side, now switch, now Alexis is taking the photo so Mom and I can have mother-daughter photos, now both daughters and Mom, now . . .

By the end, I'm starving and cranky and a little thrilled that there are only so many photos you can take with four people, instead of an entire graduating class. But today's also the first day in forever that I've gotten so many texts from friends and classmates that aren't about Mel, and for once, I'm actually responding—sending emojis and gifs to group chats I've randomly been added to, and feeling, maybe, a little more excited than usual. Then Alexis pulls up the streaming ceremony on the computer, just as we hear the doorbell ring.

"We have to go outside," Mom trills, and suddenly I'm ushered to the door, and then out the door, where I see Mel and Olivia standing, wearing masks. They're both in the middle of the front yard, another bouquet of flowers between them, along with a giant white bear in Mel's arms. Mel is wearing her high school sweatshirt, since we graduated from the same one, and when I turn around, I realize Alexis has put hers on too.

"Mel!" I screech and run toward her. I only remember myself when I'm about a foot in front of her and then I back up quickly. "Right, yes, quarantine." I don't know if this actually still counts as quarantining, but I think we're all winging it at this point. Instead of hugging her, I bounce on my heels. "Hi," I say, and it comes out high-pitched and airy. "Wait, is this safe? Are you safe? Because I know you're tired, and recovering, and maybe you should—"

"I'm good, sis." Above her mask, I can see the crinkles in the corners of her eyes that show she's smiling, and I'm willing to believe her, because she *looks* good. Still a little tired, maybe, but whatever I imagined her as in the hospital is a far cry from how she looks now, dressed in her own clothes, color in her warm brown skin as she stands nonchalantly with her arm around Olivia's waist. Olivia, for her part, looks happy, too, her long blond micro-braids tied in a high ponytail, complementing the dark green maxi dress she's wearing. It helps replace the image I have of the tearstained face and rumpled clothes she wore the first night Mel was in the hospital, when Dad insisted she stay in Mel's old room, instead of panicking alone in the apartment they share together.

The memory jars me into a sour mood. It reminds me that things might be okay on the surface, but who knows what's really going on beneath? The mental pictures I have of Mel pallid in the hospital and Alexis's fingernails, bloodied from her anxious picking, flash across my mind; I remember the concerned way Dad looked at me for days on end, the days Mom didn't leave her room. I remember that Mel is here, and I'm grateful, *so* grateful, but Drew isn't, even with the few texts between us. This could have been the one thing we shared together, even if we couldn't share it with our classmates, but we can't, because of me.

"The ceremony is starting," I manage to choke out. "Do we want to watch it out here?" Mom sprints inside and Alexis follows. A moment later, Alexis brings out my phone, so I can live-text with Colby, and a chair to put between us all. Mom puts the laptop on it so we can see. Then we sit, spread out in a circle in the grass, and watch as my high school career ends on-screen.

Mel and Olivia go home once Mom is finished taking a few hundred more photos, and then we have a dinner of Chinese food and cake, courtesy of two different delivery drivers. When we're satiated, I return upstairs. Before I take off my cap and gown, I snap a couple more selfies to send to Colby. She responds with heart eyes, and a picture of her blowing a kiss. I take off my cap and fluff out my hair, before responding with a slightly more attractive photo of myself.

Then, before I can psych myself out, I send the first picture—with the cap—to Drew. He responds more quickly than I expected, with a pic of his own. He's in a cap and gown, too, and his mom is kissing his cheek. His eyes are squinting, and his lip is curled, but his arm is around her, while the other hand is holding his framed diploma.

Congratulations.

You too.

[. . .]

Can we hang tonight?

My heart almost falls out of my chest. I desperately want to say yes, but I have six days until I can actually hug Mel again, so, reluctantly, I decline.

I understand, he says. And then he calls.

"Hey," I say when I pick up.

"Hey," he says.

"How's Robbie?" I ask. It seems like as good an icebreaker as any.

"Good," he says. "We're planning something else soon, but uh . . . the principal had the students who posted about black rifles matter and stuff apologize to us. On a video call anyway. They refused to put it in writing. But I guess that's something."

"Wow," I say, genuinely impressed and a little disappointed about the video call. I realize I might've liked to hear it. I guess that's what I get for not being involved. "I didn't think the school would actually respond," I say instead.

"Yeah. I mean, that's why sometimes it's important to speak up, you know. Even when you think it's not gonna do anything."

Sure, fine. But this isn't what I want to talk about right now. "I miss you," I say instead. "Thanks for calling."

"Yeah, well. I miss you too. And today is graduation and all, so. Didn't feel right to not talk."

I slump onto my bed and then lie on my back. "Agreed. How are you?"

"Fine," he sighs. "You know. I got an email today from UC Irvine, confirming the online schedule for first semester."

"That's fun," I say. "They have great timing."

"Yeah. I was hoping they'd wait to announce whether we'd be online, but I guess people have to make plans for travel or whatever. Now they know they don't have to."

"At least we won't have to worry about roommates we hate."

"Maybe I can find a group of other first-years and send them dirty clothes and tell them I don't know how to use a washing machine. That's sort of the same thing."

"You're so weird."

"You know it," he says. We laugh a little; it's not exactly genuine, but we're trying. The idea of him being ridiculous at college reminds me of the variety show he was supposed to do this year; the one we still haven't talked about, all this time.

"I'm sorry you didn't get to do your show," I say.

He's quiet. For a moment, I wonder if he's hung up, but when I look at my phone, I see he's still on the call. Then he lets out a slow, exaggerated sigh. "I'll live," he says. "Honestly, I've been grateful for it. I've been able to focus on other stuff. Been reading a lot. Before this past month, I thought theater would be my main focus when we got to college, but now I don't know. There's a lot of things I could do."

I breathe hard through my nose, pushing through the anxiety this line of conversation has given me the last few weeks. Try to be a good friend and just listen as he tells me about all the amazing activism he's going to pursue. "Like what?" I try to say it with enthusiasm.

"Like basket weaving," he answers, and I bark out a gasp of laughter.

"What?"

"What?" he echoes. "This shit is exhausting, man. It's important, and I'm proud to be speaking up, but I'm tired. And being onstage is different, you know, but also, just as exposing, in a way. I feel like I'm constantly on display, just by being Black and alive, and then I've been doing all these protests, and I'm not mad at it, but also, I'm low-key like . . . happy that the first semester is online? So, I can just be home, and with my family. Is that terrible?"

I inhale sharply, which is the only thing that keeps me from wanting to smack myself. All this time, I've been acting like Drew is superman and feeling guilty that I couldn't match his superpowers. But of course, he's tired too. He's human.

"No, it's not terrible," I say finally. "It makes complete and total sense." I bite my lip for a moment. "I'm sorry I haven't been there for you. Like, doing protests and stuff along with you. Do you think I'm a terrible person?"

My heart pounds as I wait for his response, bracing myself for the truth. For the answer I've been dreading for weeks: that I've completely and utterly disappointed him.

"I don't think you're terrible," he says slowly. "I think . . . you're tired." He laughs. "I mean, everything with your sister . . . I'm sorry if I've been pushing too hard. I wasn't trying to pressure you. I just wanted you to see it, you know?"

"See what?"

"That you're not alone." I hear him shift on the phone. "That's what gives me energy anyway. Seeing folks outside, chanting, and walking together, and pushing for something bigger than ourselves. It's like . . . yeah, we're speaking truth to power, but it's also what keeps me from thinking I'm the only one in the world who sees how fucked up everything is. It helps me see that other people see it, too . . . and that we're fighting back."

I nod to myself. I think of that person at the pet store who was recording the angry woman who screamed at Colby, or the fact that I was there and able to do something, say something, while Colby waited for her boss to appear. I think about how Alexis called me to visit, because her husband had to leave. I think of the fact that I was able to escape to Alexis's house, because I didn't want to be home. I think of the party Colby and I went to, because at the end of the day, we didn't want to be alone, either—in sadness, and grief, and terror. In every moment of darkness this year has brought, what has saved each of us is the willingness to reach across the empty expanse and hope that someone will reach back. Maybe Mel forgot that. But I know that no matter what, I will keep reaching, to make sure she knows it. I want Drew to know it too.

"How's Colby?" he asks.

Damn. Maybe I've been too quiet. He's reaching for something else now.

"She's—I mean, she's good."

"Tell me about her."

I groan. "Drew."

"It's all good," he says. "I mean." I hear him breathe deep. In. Out. "All you had to say was that you weren't into it," he said. "Or me, I guess. My feelings wouldn't have been hurt."

"Really?"

"No, man, not really." He laughs. "But like, it's cool. I would've preferred you talked to me about it, though, instead of like . . . ghosting me."

"I didn't ghost you. We were still talking all the time."

"Yeah, but not about the shit that counted. I had no idea what you were feeling, and then all of sudden, you're in San Diego, and then you're sneaking out, and now you're dating someone. And a girl someone, at that. At least I told you I liked boys. I didn't know you liked girls."

"I wasn't sure," I tell him. "I mean, you're the only boy I've really thought I liked, and then . . ."

"Woooow," he says. "So, I'm a terrible kisser. This is good intel for me."

"You're a great kisser," I say, which feels like a weird thing to tell your platonic best friend, but this has been a conversation waiting to happen. "It just made me realize that I don't want to kiss boys. In general. Not just you. I should've told you that sooner. I'm sorry."

"Damn," he says again. "And meanwhile, you made me realize I was bi. That's so unfair." I can't help it. I laugh before I can stop myself. But I think that's what he intended, because he's laughing too. And it's wonderful, knowing how easily we can still laugh together, after everything. That's why I know I'm not done with my apologies.

"I really am sorry," I say. "For not saying anything before. And for being so distant and weird. You deserved better."

"Thanks for saying that," he whispers. He's quiet

for another moment and then he says, "So. Have you kissed Colby yet?"

"Oh, we don't have to talk about that," I say.

"I don't mind," he says. "I mean, this is how we start again, right? By talking about the hard stuff and not running away from it. So, go for it."

At first, I'm not sure if I believe him. If I should try to gently steer the conversation to a new topic. But then again, I guess I have to trust him. After all, he's still trusting me, despite everything. "Okay," I say. "Yes. Colby and I have kissed."

"And it was . . . ?"

The sigh I give him is disgustingly blissful. I'm almost embarrassed. "It was great," I say.

"Gay."

"I know!"

"So, is she your girlfriend now?"

"No," I say. "I told her I had to tell my best friend first."

"Ha ha!" Drew exclaims, and I imagine him pumping his fist in the air. "Cosmic justice. Cool, cool, cool, cool, cool, cool, cool. So, I get final say?"

"I mean, I wouldn't go that far."

"I mean, but I would, though, is the thing. Bros before hoes, and all that."

"Oh my God, Drew."

We start laughing again until he sobers suddenly. "But even though she lives in another city and stuff, you're gonna try? Like, long distance or something?"

"We haven't really talked about it, but I think so."

He's silent for a minute. "Can I meet her?"

I hold my breath. It feels like a big question—like he's asking me to bridge the gap between the person he knew before San Diego and the one since. I didn't think there was a gap, actually, until now.

I run my tongue along my teeth, feeling the ridges while I consider. What if Drew meets Colby and sees some flaw I've ignored in the haze of our three-day in-person courtship? What if Colby meets Drew, and suddenly I'm forced to see him through someone else's eyes? What if she sees something she doesn't like, and I end up agreeing? The thought makes my stomach churn. I really, really don't like the idea, and that makes me feel like a truly terrible person. But I've said no to pretty much every other request Drew has made in the last few weeks. The least I can do is introduce him to the one situation I've let myself say yes to.

"Okay," I say. "After quarantine is over. I'll talk to Colby."

"Okay," he says. Then, "You know I love you, right?"

"I know," I say.

"No, like . . ." Drew clears his throat. "Not romantically. I mean, like, it's above that. You're my best friend, and I love you. Okay?"

I squeeze my eyes shut, certain I'm going to cry again, because I've needed to hear that for God knows how long. And it occurs to me that he needs to hear it too.

"I love you too," I say. "Always."

"Good," he says. "Glad that's settled."

And it's sort of silly, how simple that statement is, but he's right. If nothing else makes sense this year, at least we've got that figured out. At least we've got that to keep us going.

CHAPTER TWENTY-TWO

MY FAMILY BREAKS QUARANTINE AFTER another week passes. It feels both momentous and terrifying. Mel and I have now talked a bunch since she's been home, and I even saw her at graduation, but . . . I don't know. What if she's different when we're actually talking alone, in person? Or I am? It strikes me that maybe she could be a spectral version of herself—body snatched by whatever a near-death experience does to your psyche, so she only looks and sounds like my Mel but is actually someone completely different.

Mom and Dad go to see her first. They bring groceries Mom ordered from a local store and pack the car with various knickknacks that Mom stress-bought for Mel when Mel was still in the hospital, like masks decorated with Mel's favorite childhood cartoons, and a

Betty Boop lunch pail Mel once asked for when she was ten, at least according to Dad. He and Mom give Alexis and me big hugs like they're leaving for a decade and then pile into their huge white pickup truck.

Alexis keeps me busy by asking if I want to play *Overwatch* in Dad's man cave. She disdains first-person shooter games—probably with good reason—but after about an hour of putzing around, cursing out her character for misfiring, and growing ever more enraged each time she dies, suddenly her score begins to shoot up higher than mine. I wouldn't say I'm that competitive, but I have played this game many more times than Alexis. I can't let her surpass the novice level in less than a day.

We're screaming, at the screen and at each other, by the time Dad and Mom come home a few hours later. "Of course, help yourself," Dad says, when he opens the door and finds us perched on the edge of his couch, feral looks in both our eyes. We spare him a glance and then keep playing until the level is cleared.

"Boom!" Alexis shouts, slamming the controller down and then jumping up with pride. I roll my eyes, but I'm grinning. We make a good team. She sits back down and turns the game off with the remote she dropped. Then she turns her attention to Dad, who is still standing in the doorway, shaking his head with kind amusement. "So," Alexis says, suddenly a normal human person again. "How's Mel?"

Dad sighs and runs a hand over his face. "Okay. I mean, you know, it'll take time for her to really feel like herself again, but Olivia's been taking wonderful care of her."

"Has she been taking care of herself?"

Dad and Alexis both look at me, like the question I've just asked is loaded with barbed wire. Then Dad gives me a weary smile. "She's doing her best."

"How's Mom?" Alexis asked.

"She cried," Dad says. The admission itself is said lightly, almost like he'd said it was Tuesday, or that the sun was out. "But, you know, she was happy to see your sister in person, and actually be able to hug her, and to help out with the groceries, and all that. It's good. We're gonna be okay." Dad nods like he's trying to convince himself. "You're gonna go over and see her tonight?" He directs this question to Alexis.

"Yeah," she says. "We're gonna order sushi and watch a movie."

I'm a little annoyed at this. I don't know why the two of us wouldn't go together. Not for the first time, I remember that Mel and Alexis technically grew up together–before me. Without me. That fact, in this instance, makes me feel bitter and ignored, even if I don't know that I have the right to be. "And you and Mel are going somewhere tomorrow, right?" Alexis continues, looking at me.

I nod but don't say anything. History has shown I can be a little too off the cuff when I'm upset.

Dad nods too. "Good. Great." He rubs his hands together. "I'm going to go check on your mom. Y'all have fun in MY"—he points to himself aggressively—"office."

"We will," Alexis sings back.

I don't feel like playing anymore. I'm about to tell Alexis this, but she shoves the controller back in my hand and turns the screen back on. Still, I'm about to call it a day when she says, "I could probably beat this level without you, if you're tired."

Oh. She's good.

I sit back and let the game begin.

Mel picks me up around ten the next morning, and we sit in comfortable silence as we drive to one of the local nature reserves. Our quarantine might be over, but the pandemic rages on, so there aren't a ton of other places to go. Besides, walking in nature feels like a healthier alternative to an outdoor shopping mall right now anyway.

When we arrive, the sun is still low and the air is cool as we pull our small hiking bags out of the car and slather on sunscreen. We exchange small talk as we begin our walk, our sneakers becoming scuffed in loose brown sand as hikers pass by with strollers, and walking sticks, and mountain bikes.

When the sun begins to strike the highest point above us, Mel asks if I'm hungry.

"Yes, please," I say. I was too anxious to eat this morning, and I've only had an orange and a few sips from my water bottle, so actually, I'm starving. Mel leads me off the path to a grove of trees, whose thick trunks are wound up and around like dancers posing at the end of a complicated performance. I'm grateful for the privacy. A lot of people have been staring at us like freaks for covering our faces outside. I guess I got used to the expectation to wear a mask in San Diego, but it's not like that here. I think back to Parakeet Man's conversation with his birds and wonder if our fellow hikers think we've fallen prey to the *plan*demic.

We pull out the sandwiches we packed. Mel climbs onto a sturdy limb that's thick and unyielding while I cross my legs on top of a tangle of roots, leaning against the trunk beneath her. We eat in silence, listening to the footsteps that pass us by and the rustle of wind through the leaves. A couple of birds begin to sing slowly at first, until their sweetness turns severe, like there's a standoff or a marital squabble. It reminds me of the parakeets—unruly and unwelcome, but somehow comforting, after a while. Like they're reminding you that life exists in both the silence and the noise.

"I wonder how Parakeet Man is doing," I say, and Mel struggles to keep the peanut butter and jelly sandwich she was chewing in her mouth.

"He still lives there?"

"Yeah." I sigh. "Very much so."

"Good for him," Mel says. "The parakeets are keeping him alive and well."

"I guess everyone needs some kind of company," I say. "Since he lives alone. I think."

"Loneliness is one precursor to premature death." Mel takes another bite of her sandwich, and I use the opportunity to open my big mouth.

"Were you lonely?"

There it is. The thing I've been building up the courage to bring up all day. Everyone's still really delicate about it. Well, I'm sure Mel's talked about it with my parents, or with Alexis. But no one's talked about it *with me*. No one's talked about what Mel is going to do next. Or why she did it to begin with.

Mel swallows and puts the sandwich down. She closes her eyes. "In a way, I guess."

"Aren't you happy with Olivia?"

She opens her eyes again and keeps them on the sky. They track a bird that flies above us and disappears past the canopy. "I'm thrilled with Olivia. Wouldn't trade her for anything."

"Except death, apparently."

Mel snorts, like what I said was hilarious. I don't think it's very funny. She slides off the tree's long limb and then sits down beside me.

"I've always struggled with this, you know? Since I was a kid. I think it's just worse in some people than in others."

"But why now? I feel like you were doing great and then all of a sudden . . ."

"I watched that video." Mel looks down at her hands. "Of those police officers, and George Floyd. I didn't mean to; it's not like I was looking for it. It just popped up, and like . . ." Her fingers close. Open. Close again. "You try so hard sometimes, in the world. To do all the right things. Wake up early, go to work, pay your rent, call your parents. Eat right, speak right, breathe right. And then, you see something like that, and it feels like, what's the point? Why bother? They're gonna kill us anyway. It's just a matter of when."

It's my turn to look down. "So, you just decided to give up."

"Honestly, it was kind of an accident. I don't feel like I decided anything. I took a pill, and then another, and then I woke up in the hospital."

There's something scratching at my throat. It's clawing, deep and desperate, and burning the skin as I push it down, down, down.

"Okay," I say.

Mel puts her arm around me, and I let her, though my body is stiff. "Alexis told me about another protest tonight in San Diego. I guess one of her council members said something dumb; I don't know. But we're gonna go, together."

"What? Why?" I pull away to look at her face. She seems surprised.

"I thought you'd be happy. I'm going to show up, add my voice to the crowd. Better than giving up, right?"

"But you could get hurt, or arrested, or . . . something."

Mel laughs, but it's incredulous. "I mean, yeah, but it wouldn't be my first rodeo. I've been to, like, a lot of protests in my life. Too many, honestly."

"And how many of them actually mattered?"

"Seriously?"

"Why can't you just stay home and spend time with Olivia, or, like, I don't know, be happy that you're *not* dead and stop trying to get someone else to finish the job?" I'm attempting not to yell, but my chest is heaving with the effort, because what I really want to do is scream.

"Whoa, whoa." Mel puts her hands up. "I see that you're feeling some kind of way. Why don't we talk about that, instead of throwing stones?"

"I'm feeling fine," I say, and stand, wiping off my jeans. I throw our food back into our backpacks and walk to the main path. "Can we go? I wanna finish the loop before it gets too hot."

Mel follows me, and I spend the rest of our hike pretending that she's not looking at me the way our parents have often looked at her: like there's something they wish they could fix, but they have absolutely no idea where to begin.

CHAPTER TWENTY-THREE

WHEN MEL DROPS ME OFF AT HOME, I FIND Dad in his office. This time, he's not on the couch playing a game, but on his keyboard, working out a tune and humming, just like Alexis. I knock, to tell him I'm at the door, and he gives me a thumbs-up with a huge grin, a sign that I can interrupt his work. I give him a tight hug, and he hugs me back. "How's Mel?" he asks.

I look for the concern beneath his words, like maybe he's wanting me to say how Mel *really* is, and not how Mel appears. But the words are innocuous. He's looking at me like he expects a straightforward answer.

"Mel is fine," I say. "Allegedly."

"Mm," he says. "Are you worried that she's not really fine?"

"Well, yeah. Aren't you?"

"I'm always worried for y'all."

"Sure. Because you're our dad. But I mean, like, because she has depression too. You know she's planning to go to a protest with Alexis?"

"That's probably a good thing," Dad muses. He squints his eyes at me and then takes off his headphones, like that will somehow help him see me better. "I'm guessing you don't agree."

"I feel like this whole thing is what triggered the hospital stay to begin with. Wouldn't surrounding yourself with despair and rage be, like, the opposite next step to take?"

"Didn't Drew hold a protest recently?"

I frown. How did he hear about that?

"I read it in the *OC Register*," Dad responds to the question I must have on my face. "And your school newsletter said that the students and teachers came to an amicable conclusion."

I forget sometimes that my parents have that kind of surveillance. I cross my arms. "That's what Drew said, yeah."

"So, sometimes, protests can be helpful. They can lead to good outcomes."

"Or bad ones."

Dad nods thoughtfully. "Sometimes. But if people

hadn't protested, no one would even know Mr. Floyd's name, besides his family."

"He had a group of people around him, filming, and he still died."

Dad closes his eyes. Nods. Sighs. Rubs his face. He turns away from his keyboard, to give me his full attention. "A lot of our people die. And it's not fair. And it gets tiring, it gets bone-deep exhausting. Makes you not want to fight back."

To give up, I think. Like Mel tried to.

"But that's what they want from you. I mean, that's what the bigger powers want. They want us to shut up, sit down, roll over. They want us to be too tired to push back."

"And they keep killing us."

"And after four hundred years, we're still here." Dad reaches out to touch my hand, but I pull away. I hear what he's saying, but it's hard to accept. I guess it's a glass half empty or half full kind of thing. You can look at four hundred years of hardship and be proud of how far you've come, or you can look it and realize you're still fighting different shades of the same battle.

Drew is the type of person who's willing to keep fighting. Mel, for a moment, wasn't. And me? I guess I haven't decided on the person I am yet.

CHAPTER TWENTY-FOUR

SINCE MEL AND ALEXIS ARE GOING BACK TO San Diego tonight, I figure it's as good a time as any for Drew to meet Colby too. They both agree when I text them, despite the short notice, and Drew asks for a late afternoon retrieval. Alexis and I pick up Mel first, parking outside her apartment complex while some emo band my sisters loved in high school blares out of the speakers at top volume. Mel shuffles through her front door and hops into the passenger seat, wedging her backpack with overnight supplies between her legs. I don't know if she forgives me for this morning, or if I need her to, but she doesn't seem to be letting it get to her. Instead, she reaches for me in the back seat and gives me a quick but firm side hug, before launching into a recount of the podcast she and Olivia are currently bingeing.

As we drive, Alexis and Mel keep things light and I lean my head against the back seat window, tapping my fingers gently on the leather seats as we get closer and closer to Drew's house. I'm hoping that things will feel normal. Or at least, not painfully awkward. He and I have been on a good wavelength since graduation, but I still haven't seen him in person. So, when we finally pull up to his house, I nearly jump in surprise. He's already outside, and now he's walking up to Alexis's car, wearing a faded *Wicked* hoodie and a plain black cap that pushes his curls down into his eyes. His hands are tucked into the pockets of his jeans, which are pulled over his clean, black Timbs. He must be taking this meeting with Colby seriously—he only pulls out the Timbs on special occasions. I wonder if he wore them for graduation.

Alexis opens her car door and pulls him in for a long hug, which he accepts. Mel gives him a dap when he slides in next to me, and he and I do the same before buckling our seat belts. He looks good: different, a little, but not much. Older, maybe, but not unrecognizable. Still the person I love, who loves me. We settle in beside each other, arms and shoulders touching comfortably. All four of us are wearing black face masks, but Drew's has the words *Black Lives Matter* stitched across in white lettering. It makes me hope that no one can see inside the car, or that we're not stopped by police, and then I feel ashamed.

"Can you turn on some music?" I pose the question to the front seat, and Alexis starts pressing buttons as Mel turns around.

"Fine," Mel says, "but we're not listening to Barbra, Celine, or Lin-Manuel Miranda."

"How about Beyoncé?" Alexis suggests.

"Perfect!" Drew exclaims.

We start with *I Am . . . Sasha Fierce* and end the drive with *Lemonade*, all of us singing along to "Formation" about half a dozen times before we finally pull up to Alexis's apartment an hour and a half later. I point out Parakeet Man's apartment to Drew as we pass, and Houston greets us all at the front door. He's tall and muscular, wearing a simple black sweater and blue jeans, with a mop of tousled brown hair that's due for a haircut. When he sees his wife, he pulls her into a tight embrace, like he's been desperate for her to return. Probably, he has been. They share a sweet kiss, and it's confirmation that Alexis is taken care of, even when I don't see her all the time.

Houston gives Drew a quick hug, too, since they've met a few times over the years, and then a longer hug for me. But when he sees Mel, his smile wobbles. Suddenly, he wraps both of his tan arms around her and lifts her into the air. It's a little amusing to see this tall white man lift my short and curvy brown-skinned sister in the air like his long-lost twin, but Mel was Alexis's maid of honor at her wedding. She's known Houston a long time. I bet he was as worried as we all were. When Houston sets her down, he stands up straight and blows out a breath, wiping his eyes free of tears as he turns away.

"Okay, inside, everyone. I made dinner," he announces.

"Thank God," Mel says.

We step inside and Poirot launches at me first. Without meaning to, I coo at him with abandon and hold him close to my chest, my body hunched over his. He rubs his wet nose against my cheek and I'm only just barely able to keep him from licking my entire face. I missed his wriggly body, and smushed face, and no-longer-off-putting puppy smell. I hate to say it, but yes: I have finally succumbed to the fur prince's powerful puppy enchantment. And I feel great about it.

Then he seems to realize his mom is home, which means nothing else in the world matters. He squeaks out excited barks and runs around Alexis, then at her, then into her arms, and she laughs, and I laugh, and Drew and Mel both look at me like I'm someone they're meeting for the first time. It's not bad. Just different.

Soon, Poirot doesn't seem to know whether he wants to chase his tail, scratch his ear, eat the carpet, or continue getting pets from the host of people who have just entered his home. Mel leans down and pets him behind the ear, and Drew gives his belly a good rub, before Houston and Alexis finally usher us into the kitchen.

"So, let me get this straight," Houston says as he takes a bite of lasagna. "Drew gets to meet your new girlfriend before your family does?"

"You haven't met her?" Mel asks Alexis.

"Nope," she responds. "Sure haven't."

"Does that mean we get to crash your interrogation?" Mel asks Drew.

"It's not an interrogation," I say, at the same time that Drew says, "I don't see why not." I glare at him. "Okay, we are not converging on Colby like SEAL Team Six," I assert. "I just want my best friend and my . . . new friend . . . to meet. You guys can meet her later."

"Once I approve," Drew clarifies. He winks at me, and I toss a sprinkle of parmesan in his general direction.

"So, you aren't going to the protest, then, right?" Houston directs this question to both of us, and I feel heat rise to my cheeks.

"What protest?" Drew asks.

"The local council is trying to impose a curfew, so

that folks *can't* protest after work, which is the most accessible time for people," Alexis says.

"So, we're protesting their attempt to squash the protests," Houston adds.

"That's meta," I mutter.

"Maybe we can go after," Drew suggests. He raises an eyebrow at me, and I keep focusing on my lasagna. He looks at Houston. "Are you going?"

"Of course," Houston says. "That's not even a question."

Awesome. Even the white guy is going. "We're going to be late," I say to Drew. "Are you almost done?"

He takes another bite and then downs a cup of water. "Ready," he sings as he grabs his hoodie from the back of his chair and tugs it over his head. "Let's meet wifey."

"We'll probably be at the protest by the time you guys get back," Alexis calls.

"I still have the spare key," I assure Alexis as Drew follows me out the door, singing the lyrics to Jagged Edge's "Let's Get Married" and reminding me, not for the first time, that this is probably a terrible idea.

CHAPTER TWENTY-FIVE

AS WE WALK TOWARD THE PARK WHERE WE'RE planning to meet Colby, Drew looks around, his expression one of total awe. "So many of these stores have a BLM sign on them," he says. "It's way different than Irvine." I nod. I want to say something dismissive, but I feel the same way he does, I bet: seen and safer for it, instead of the opposite. God, I missed this place.

Suddenly, Drew stops. At first, I just see a Latino man with a handlebar mustache and a thick paintbrush, dripping color onto the mottled white canvas at his feet as he stares up at the wall in front of him. Then I see it: two huge black-and-white portraits on the wall, towering over us like saints in a cathedral. One is of a young Black woman with round cheeks and smiling eyes beneath a wave of pressed black hair. Under her portrait are the words *Breonna Taylor, March 13, 2020.*

Next to her is the portrait of a Black man, much older than the woman. His body is at an angle, like he's leaning away from whoever captured his image, but his lips are curved ever so slightly. Like he might be smiling, if you looked long enough. Beneath him are the words *George Floyd, May 25, 2020.*

The portrait is based on that photo we've all seen shared on the news and online. The only image I've ever seen of him alive. But there must be others. Ones that have never been shared with the public. What must it be like, I wonder, to have the entirety of your existence—your capacity for love and humor, heartbreak and fear, the essence of your humanity—reduced to one photo? That's my first thought, pulsing and painful as it knocks about in my brain.

My second is that I've never heard of the younger woman.

"Do you know who she is?" I ask Drew.

He looks at me incredulously. "Yeah," he says. "She was killed by police too. They were investigating a drug deal or something and forced entry into her house. Her boyfriend thought they were intruders, so he fired a warning shot, and then they fired back, like, thirty times."

"And the boyfriend survived?"

"Yeah."

"But she . . ."

Drew shakes his head and I go back to staring at her image, a woman who looks so similar to me or Mel. How many other deaths haven't I heard of? How many people die whose names I will never know?

A few people have joined us on the sidewalk, watching as the man puts up finishing touches on his artwork. Drew touches my arm, and we keep walking.

When we reach the park, Colby waves at us from beneath a skinny tree, its leaves providing just enough shade for the picnic blanket she's sitting on, although with the sun beginning to set, we won't need it soon. She jogs over to us and nearly throws her arms around my neck, before she seems to realize Drew may not approve. Instead, she stops in front of me and sticks out her hand. I shake it awkwardly and Drew turns around like he's ready to walk away. "Y'all gotta be kidding me," he says.

I wink at Colby before I pull her to me and press a

kiss beneath her ear. She giggles with a hand over her mouth and presses her forehead against mine. She smells like vanilla and rose water. My knuckles rub against the fabric of her T-shirt, up and down, and she moves her head to my neck.

"Wow, it's like that?" Drew says, now facing us with his arms crossed.

Blushing, Colby and I pull away from each other. "Drew," I say, "this is Colby."

Colby puts her hand out, and Drew bends, lifting her hand to his lips. "Nice to meet the famous Colby," he says. He lets her hand go and stands up straight. "I'm Drew, the best friend. Tia and I kissed once, but I think she likes kissing you more."

Colby looks at me with wide eyes, which is probably similar to the look I'm giving Drew. "I—yeah. He's bi," I say. "Was gay. But. Now bi."

"Probably was always bi," Drew clarifies.

Colby nods slowly, like she's processing all this information she didn't ask for. "Okay," she says. "Uh. Me too." She nods at Drew. "Nice to meet you."

Drew bows with a flourish of the hands. "So," he says, "shall we sit?"

Twenty minutes later, Colby is listening intently as Drew recounts the adventures of our ninth-grade summer, when I tried to learn how to kayak and then accidentally capsized our boat, because I got excited when a seal swam past.

"You were terrified," Drew corrects me.

"I was not!" My arm is around Colby and she's leaning against me as we talk.

"You said, *Drew, there's a demon in the water.*"

"I didn't realize it was a seal."

"To be fair, who knows their true forms," Colby chimes in. "They could be both."

Drew runs his finger over his chin like he's considering the proposition. "You know, that's very true."

Colby gets a call from her dad, and she walks away to talk to him. Drew leans over to me. "I like her," he says.

"Really?"

"Yeah," he says. "And I can tell you like her too."

"I do."

"Then it's official. Give me your hand." I do, and he gives me three daps, one to my knuckle, then above and below. "You have my permission to date."

"I wasn't asking permission!"

"Yeah, you were," he says, leaning on his palms as Colby walks back toward us.

Yeah. I was.

"It's getting late," Colby says. "My mom is getting worried." She shoots me an apologetic glance. "I told her about what happened at the beach, and now she's like a hundred times more concerned about the probability of my imminent death, so she's been more obsessive about making sure I'm home at a reasonable time. Dad's doing his best, but I should probably head home soon."

"Fuck that guy," Drew says. "I mean, the guy at the beach. Not your dad. I'm sorry you experienced that."

Colby shrugs. "It happens," she says, and he sighs as he stands.

"Yeah. I know."

We help her pack the picnic blanket in her tote bag, and Colby offers to drive us back to Alexis's house. Drew graciously allows me to take shotgun, and as we drive, Colby puts on some sort of heavy metal album, which is kind of terrifying but genuinely only makes me like her more. As she navigates the streets, we pass by the mural portraits again.

"When did they start putting those up?" I ask her.

Colby checks her mirror and makes a sound of recognition. "About a week ago," she says.

"I'd never heard of the other person. Breonna," I say.

Colby looks at me, and I can feel Drew looking at us both. Colby reaches out and puts her hand on my thigh. "It's hard to keep track sometimes. But you've heard of her now."

Drew pipes up from behind me. "That's what matters."

And I wonder if they're right. If the important thing is at least knowing, even when the knowing feels like too much to bear. I wonder how many lives have to end before we finally forget. I think about what my dad said and wonder if that's the point.

A few more turns and then we're on Alexis's street again. Except this time, people are blocking the road as they crowd around half a dozen police cars with flashing red lights and the blare of sirens.

CHAPTER TWENTY-SIX

COLBY TRIES TO HONK, BUT THE CROWD doesn't budge.

"Can you back up?" Drew asks. Colby looks behind her, but another car has already tried to turn onto the street. It honks, too, repeatedly.

"I'm gonna put my hazards on," she says. She pulls the car as far to the side of the road as she can, and the car behind her tries to pull forward before the driver realizes that it can't. More cars are piling up behind it.

Colby turns her car off, and we exit slowly, craning our necks to try to see through the crowd. Alexis and Mel didn't say the protest was literally on their street, but I guess I could've misunderstood. Yet I don't hear any chants, or see any posters waving through the air. Instead, people are muttering to themselves and each other, and their phones are out, lifted high above their heads, recording. I realize they're not protesters.

They're witnesses.

"Excuse me," I say as we squeeze past. "I live on this street, so I'm just trying . . ." People move to let us pass, but they're focused on the scene in front of them, and soon I see why. Two men are in the middle of the street, brawling. One is white and one is Black and that's about all I can tell, as they claw at each other with spit and curses flying from their mouths. Two police officers, a Black woman and an Asian man, are trying to grab the men without being pulled into the vortex, as other officers urge the crowd to give them space and not engage.

"What happened?" Drew asks an Asian woman, who's typing rapidly on her phone.

She points to a car parked right in front of Alexis's complex. I recognize it as the one that had the BLACK BABIES MATTER sign taped to the back passenger side window. Except now the window is shattered. Shards of glass cover the ground, as if someone threw a rock through it.

"The white guy broke the Black guy's mirror," she says. She continues typing rapidly. I look over her shoulder; she's posting updates to social media, providing details about the police officers on-site, including their badge numbers.

Another police officer, a white man, joins the fray, and with the three of them, they're able to pry the men apart. Both men are bleeding, and ragged, collars torn and shoes missing. At first they seem limp, like the fight's been taken out of them, but then one takes a swing at the female police officer in an attempt to get free, and a gun is drawn.

The crowd gasps, someone screams, and then suddenly, it's like we're pushing forward, individual bodies turned into a mass that moves as one.

"It's a taser," the white police officer shouts, but I don't think the crowd hears him. Instead, people finally start to chant. *We're watching you! We're watching you! We're watching you!*

Colby reaches for me and I catch her hand, hoping my grip is tight and reassuring. It's almost laughable, the fact that we're here right now. All this time, I've been avoiding this very thing, and yet here I am, whether I want to be or not. And yet I don't move. I could—Alexis's house is right there. We could be safe inside, in no time, and yet . . .

I may not be able to stop what's happening, but I can make sure people *know* that it's happening.

I can be a witness too.

I reach for Drew's hand, but he's not there. He's ahead of us, moving forward, bobbing like a boat on rocky waves, his phone high, his words clear. *We're watching! We're watching!*

As the crowd grows more restless, I hear car doors shutting behind us. It's probably more people trying to get home, who don't know what they're in for. At least, that's what I assume; that's what makes sense.

What doesn't make sense is the screech of tires, the screams, and the headlights that flash like a bright wave, showcasing my best friend's young and terrified face as a car speeds toward him.

CHAPTER TWENTY-SEVEN

525,600 MINUTES MAKE UP AN ENTIRE YEAR.

How many minutes take up a moment that feels like a year?

Or a lifetime?

Or a single breath?

Is he breathing?

Can I breathe?

I can't breathe. I can't . . .

CHAPTER TWENTY-EIGHT

"BREATHE."

I'm holding Drew's hand, and counting for him, as he inhales and exhales. Someone has given him their coat. He's shaking, but I don't think he's cold. Colby is crouched beside him, offering him a bottle of water that someone else handed us. I don't know where it came from. In the distance, the Asian woman from before is talking to one of the police officers. She's giving him the license plate of the car that sped off.

"I have it on video too," someone else says.

"Me too," a chorus confirms.

The two men who started the fight are both in handcuffs. One of the cops crouches in front of us. He'd been among those officers keeping the crowd at bay.

"Hey," he says now, giving Drew a sympathetic smile. "You feeling a little steadier? Less spooked?"

Drew nods. The police officer looks at the three of us. "How old are you guys? Fifteen? Sixteen?"

"We're seventeen," I tell him.

"Do you need me to call a parent? Take you home?"

"My older sister lives in the apartments behind us. We were trying to get home . . ."

The police officer nods. "Got it. Well, listen, a lot of these folks have the license plate of the car, so we'll find the driver in no time. If you want to make a statement, talk to your parents, and you can let me know. It's Officer Paul Rodriguez. Okay?"

Drew nods but still doesn't say anything.

Officer Rodriguez looks at me pointedly. "You've got fast reflexes, kid. You should consider sports."

"She plays volleyball." We all look at Drew, who's staring at the water bottle clutched in his hands. He hasn't said much since I pulled him away from the car. Officer Rodriguez squeezes his shoulder and stands up. After a while, Drew stands too. He slips the stranger's jacket off his shoulders and it seems to disappear back into the mass of people. Colby and I stand with him, and then he wraps his arms around me. We hold each other, thankful for every minute that passes that we're still here.

My sisters and Houston come home half an hour later. They had only just arrived at city hall when they got my call and turned the car around immediately. Mom and Dad are on their way too. Drew still hasn't called his parents, but Colby has been on the phone with hers, assuring them that she's alive, and well, and safe as she paces the living room floor. Drew and I are sitting beside each other on the couch as Poirot pulls himself up into the space between us. He releases a deep and heavy sigh as he settles in.

Drew gently rests his hand on Poirot's head. "Do you know that petting dogs reduces your stress and theirs?" he asks me quietly.

"I believe it," I respond in kind. So far, this is about all we've managed to say to each other, but my knee is touching his. Our arms brush as we both run our fingers through Poirot's soft fur, feel his tiny body heat sink into our own. We feel his life, and each other's, with every quiet breath.

A moment later, there's a knock on the door, and Houston answers.

It's Parakeet Man. As usual, he's not wearing a mask, but he is holding a tray. There's a tea kettle on top.

"I heard the ruckus," he says, his voice low and mournful as ever. "Outside my window. The birds were distressed." He pushes the tray toward Houston, who only takes it because it's already practically in his hands. "Hot tea is good for stress," he says. "Please return it when you've finished." Then he turns and disappears into the evening, like a specter retreating into the shadows.

"Wow," Mel says as Alexis takes the tray from Houston.

"This night keeps getting stranger and stranger," Alexis mutters. "I prefer coffee, but I suppose this will do." She smiles to herself. "That was nice of him."

"I guess we have to learn his name now," Houston muses as Mel and Alexis walk past him into the kitchen.

"I wouldn't go that far," Alexis calls back. From where I'm sitting, I watch as Mel reaches into the cupboard for honey while Alexis pours tea into the little teacups that Parakeet Man provided, each of them designed, unsurprisingly, with small birds. As she navigates the kitchen, it's clear that Mel probably has been here multiple times. There's a language my sisters share that I probably won't know, because they have years on me. Still, Alexis turns to me as Mel stirs in the honey and asks, "Can you clear the table?" I do, quickly, gently swatting away Colby's and Drew's hands as they try to help. Then I help Alexis as she sets down the tea kettle and cups on the coffee table. Absently, Alexis pulls me in for a hug, and I realize that the language my sisters have isn't all that secret—it's just different. Something we share with one another, unique to each of us.

When the cups are ready, we all take steady sips, our mouths filling with cardamom tea and honey that warms our throats and coats our tongues. We breathe in heat and sweetness and breathe out relief. Still, my body feels unsettled—uncertain.

I leave the teacup on the coffee table and excuse myself to Alexis's room. I don't want to be outside, but I do want to be alone. Just for a moment. I push the door closed behind me and sink onto the queen-size bed. It's pushed up against the only window in the room, huge like a picture frame in the center of the wall. I decide the streetlamps of the neighborhood outside offer enough light and don't bother with the light switch beside the bed. I just sit there. I just breathe.

I wait for the tears to come, but they don't. I wait for the fear to subside. It doesn't. I wait for the anger to dissipate, but it stays, sinking into my bones, pulsing through my skin. Drew is alive, yes, but only because I happened to be fast enough to move him. Mel is alive, yes, but only because she didn't take enough pills to kill her. Colby and I are alive, but only because that white man at the bar was probably too drunk to do much harm.

We are alive, but at any moment, for any reason, that could stop being true. Not because of the pandemic, or even because of police, specifically, but simply because we live in a world we were never meant to thrive in. The fact that we've survived seems more like an accident than a miracle.

But then my dad's words come back to me. *We're still here*, he said. And Drew's words: *We're fighting back.*

Four hundred years and what has it got us?

My family. Colby. Me.

I breathe. We are here, and we are fighting back.

It doesn't always feel like enough. But sometimes, I guess it has to be.

CHAPTER TWENTY-NINE

A FEW MINUTES LATER, SOMEONE KNOCKS on the bedroom door. Or maybe it's an hour later. I have no idea. But there's a knock, nonetheless. "Come in," I say.

I'm not looking up when the door opens, but soon after, I feel an arm wrap around me. "Hey," Mel says gently. She pulls me closer, and I let myself fall against her shoulder. "Everything's going to be okay."

"How do you know?" I whisper.

Mel laughs, low and quiet. "I guess I don't. But I bet I know how you feel. Frustrated, and angry, and maybe a little hopeless."

"Something like that."

"Yeah. I don't have any cure for that. If I did, I would've taken it a long time ago."

"Are you upset it didn't work?" The question rests between us. It was barely above a whisper, anyway, and at first, I think she'll pretend she didn't hear me. I feel her chest fill with air, and then I feel it release.

"No," she says finally. "I'm not sad the pills didn't work."

"Why not?"

She leans her head against mine. Her hand is on my arm and I feel her fingers tighten, a firm but comforting pressure against my skin. "Believe it or not, I like being here. Most of the time. I like my life and love my girlfriend. I love our parents, and Alexis. I love you." At this, she tickles me and I shriek, like a little kid. I push her away playfully and grab a pillow for revenge. She beats me to it and blocks the blow of the pillow, then goes on the offensive. Soon it's like we're sparring, pillow to pillow, her reflexes against mine. For that brief moment, that's all I focus on: Mel and me, wrenching madness from misery.

"Whoa." Drew's voice comes to us from above the noise. "Okay, good. I thought for a second y'all had come to blows."

I smack him with a pillow too.

"Oh, okay. I see how it is." He leaves, and for a moment Mel and I just wait, the rapid rush of energy we had slowly disappearing, draining back into solemnity, until suddenly Drew barrels back in, now with a new pillow from the couch, and before I can react, he keeps barreling toward me, until I've been pushed completely back, onto the bed, my body hitting the mattress as he knocks the wind out of me.

"Oof!" I say.

"Nice!" Mel says, and she and Drew trade high fives.

"Are you guys okay?" Alexis asks. She's standing in her doorway now, eyes wide in surprise and concern.

"Not at all," Mel says.

"Not even a little," Drew agrees.

"We're falling apart," I add.

"Oh, okay," Alexis says, like that makes sense. It probably does. "Well, uh, Tia, Colby has to get going . . ."

"Oh shit," I mutter, scrambling off the bed. I shuffle over to the freestanding full-length mirror beside Alexis's closet, in the corner opposite her bed, and give myself a once-over, smoothing out my wrinkled shirt and fixing my haywire twists.

As I rush pass Drew and Mel, both of them now sitting on Alexis's bed, Drew grabs my arm. He turns me around and pulls something from the back of my head, then places a piece of white fluff in front of my face.

"Thanks," I say, and then I hug him tightly. He hugs me back.

"I got you," he says.

"I know," I say.

Then I rush past Alexis and into the living room, where Colby is awkwardly waiting by the front door, her keys in her hands.

"Sorry," I say, slightly out of breath. "I shouldn't have just left you out here with my family. That was so rude."

She gives me a sweet smile and shakes her head. "Your best friend almost got hit by a car. I think I can forgive you just this once."

"Cool," I say awkwardly. "Thanks."

She nods, and for a moment, we're both quiet. Then she stretches forward and presses a lingering kiss to my mouth. "You are super brave," she says, and leans her forehead against mine. "My hero."

I don't think I'm brave—not really. But it's the second time she's called me heroic just for doing what I thought was right.

"Just acting on instinct," I whisper.

"I know," she says. "Your instincts are good."

And I don't know. Maybe she's right. Maybe I'm braver than I think I am. I may not be as brave as Drew, but I try to protect the people I love. Mel may not be as brave as Drew, either, but she's brave enough to keep trying. And maybe that's all we can ask for. Maybe that's the best we can do.

A throat clears behind us, and when Colby and I separate, Houston waves apologetically. "Sorry," he says. "You left your phone on the coffee table, and it looks like your mom is calling again." Colby curses and thanks him as she pockets her phone.

"Okay," she sighs. "I guess I gotta go."

"I'm sorry this is how we met," Alexis says now as she approaches, "but I'm glad we got to meet. You seem really lovely." She gives her a warm hug, and Houston does too. Mel and Drew appear behind him and follow with tight hugs of their own. Drew and Colby hug for a beat longer than my siblings.

"I'm glad you're safe," she says.

"Thanks," he says. "Really."

Then she disappears through the door, and I'm left with my family and Drew. We watch the rest of *Tiger King* until Dad and Mom show up two hours later.

Mom wraps her arms around Drew the second she sees him, pulling him into her bosom like her fourth child, while Dad gives the rest of us firm hugs. Drew doesn't fight Mom's embrace. Instead, he sinks into it, wrapping his arms around her waist, and letting himself be loved on, which is exactly what he deserves. After a few more seconds of her whispering into his ear how proud of him she is, and how happy she is that he's safe, she pulls him to the kitchen table and whips out her phone. A second later, I hear Drew say, "Hi, Mom," as he leans into the phone, his other hand tucked up between Poirot's chin, which is resting against his leg.

Mom comes back over to where the rest of us are gathered on the couch, now sipping on cold tea. She isn't done doling out hugs, though. She wraps her arms around all of us, although her arms aren't particularly long; Dad helps complete the circle, keeping us all huddled together. We take a breath together as one, and then we hear Poirot's high, insistent bark.

"Sorry," Drew says softly as he stands behind Poirot, a hand tucked into one of his pockets. "Can I join?"

"Boy, get in here," Dad says, his hand pulling Drew in by the back of his head, and yes, *now* we're complete. Because Drew may not be related by blood, but he *is* my family, and my sisters and my parents know that, and they love him for it too.

That night, my parents stay in Alexis and Houston's bedroom, while Alexis and Houston take the pull-out bed. They fought Drew on this, *a lot.* Pointed out he had a trauma, which is fair. But Drew insisted he's fine, and so they tried to give it to Mel, who has *also* had a trauma, but she refused, too, and then finally Mel, Drew, and I figured out a pile of blankets and pillows on the floor. (No one really insisted on taking the bedroom; my parents are old; God knows how many traumas *they've* had.)

Miraculously, sleep seems to find us all, even as Poirot climbs over each and every one of us, when he's not whining at Alexis's closed bedroom door to sniff the houseguests. Houston's snores soon rise over all the other sounds like the star of the existing ambient noise, and then I feel Drew's knee wedged into my back, while Mel's arm drapes across my chest, though she's fully facing the opposite direction. It's cramped and hot, even with the windows open and the fans whirring, and completely lacking in anything anyone might consider comfortable.

But I'm not mad at any of it.

Because I've spent almost months alternating between isolation and constant upheaval. We all have, enduring darkness that has seemed endless at times. But tonight, crammed and uncomfortable though we may be, we're together, dreaming, breathing, and well assured that in this darkness, we are each other's light.

CHAPTER THIRTY

I WAKE BEFORE THE SUN RISES. WHEN I TURN to my side, Mel is gone. I scramble to my feet as quickly as I can without waking Drew and peek into the kitchen, then the bathroom. She's not there. I tiptoe over to Alexis's body on the couch and lean over her. "Alexis," I whisper.

She grunts, and Poirot's tail wags. He's sleeping on her chest. "Alexis," I try again, a little more harshly.

"Mm?" she says, frowning, eyes closed.

"Mel's gone."

"No, she's not," Alexis mutters. I'm about to protest when Alexis turns over, letting Poirot roll unceremoniously to her side. He stretches his paws beneath her ribs as Alexis grumbles, "She's with Mom and Dad."

"Oh." Still, I need to be sure. Slowly, I tiptoe past Alexis and Houston toward their bedroom, keeping my steps quiet against the creaking of the wooden floor, which seems unusually loud tonight. When I crack open the room door there's darkness, just for a moment, but my eyes adjust, and there she is: my big sister looking small, wild curls peeking out from beneath the sheets as she lies tucked between our mom and dad, the three of them breathing in rhythm, arms wrapped around one another. I smile and gently pull the door shut.

The sun peeks through the blinds when I turn to face the living room. Quietly, I walk toward the couch, where I gently pry Poirot out from beneath Alexis. "Hey, bud," I whisper as he sneezes. "Want to go on a walk?" Suddenly, his tail thumps with anticipation. I hold back a laugh and carry him to his wall of wardrobe attire, pulling down his harness, collar, and leash. "Okay," I say. "Let's get the family some coffee, huh?"

At the last second, I remember my mask, and then that I should switch out of Alexis's pajama bottoms and into my jeans. I locate and pocket my phone. Then we walk outside, down the stairs and past Parakeet Man, who's already standing in the courtyard. Another parakeet—this time a tall and elegant one with golden yellow feathers—is perched on his shoulder while Parakeet Man holds a cup of tea. He's looking toward the sun. When he sees me, he lifts his teacup like a salute.

"A new day is coming," he says, and I give him my bravest smile.

"It is," I say.

And right now, that's what I'll keep believing.

ACKNOWLEDGMENTS

I was both honored and terrified to write this novel—in part, because we're dealing with the murders of (at least) two real, innocent people whose lives were cut short due to bias, negligence, and a lack of respect for Black lives. How do I pay my respects to them, and to their memories—these people I don't know, but whose faces have been splashed across news stations and social media posts; these people with whom I share a culture, a lineage, and the burden of history? I hope I did right by them, in some very small way. So, first, I acknowledge George Floyd and Breonna Taylor. You mattered, you matter, and you will always matter.

And from there, to Black kids, Black girls, and queer kids everywhere: I see you, I respect you, and I value you. You are one among a billion stars. That's not insignificant. You know why? Because every star—every single one—burns bright, and bold, and brilliant. Don't ever let anyone tell you otherwise.

I would never have been able to write this novel were it not for my own stars: Alex, Carrie, and Nova. Thank you for holding me, every moment of every day. For coffee, fandom shenanigans, nonsensical riddles, and reminders to sit down and open the Word doc, even when I DON'T WANNA.

Many thanks to Foyinsi Adegbonmire, my editor, for her unwavering patience, kind words, and support. This book exists because you believed I could write it. Thanks as well to my agent, Quressa Robinson, for always being in my corner and encouraging me to write the books of my heart.

Many thanks, too, to Margaret Raymo and Kwame Alexander, for seeing a light in me and always encouraging it to shine.

Thank you to Kelly Markus, Dominic Bugatto, Rich Deas, Emily Stone, Jamie Herbeck, and Courtney Jordan, for such a GORGEOUS book package and for championing this book!

And I have to thank my grandmother, who passed away while I was writing this book. I thought you'd live forever. It seems improbable that you're not here—but your spirit lives on, and as I think about your journey as a Black woman, living nearly 100 years in this country, I'm in awe and humbled. You should never have had to be courageous, and yet to thrive here, one must be. Thank you. I love you.

And to my beloved grandfather, who survives her: Thank you for continuing to be strong, and brave, and wonderful, and for coming to every major milestone of my life, from kindergarten graduation to my book events. You inspire me every day.

Thank you to my aunt and cousins (and brother-cousin), who always show such love and light in the darkest times. Thank you to my parents, for your constant love and encouragement, and to my sisters, for always laughing with me. We laugh about a lot of good things, and a lot of absurd things, but nonetheless we laugh, and that's part of what makes this life so sweet.

Finally, a shout-out to my favorite people, in no particular order: Raquel, Anthony, José, Jaz, Steph, Yolli, Leah, Heather—you guys are genuinely the best. Thank you for being my family.

ABOUT THE AUTHOR

GEORGIA K. BOONE is the author of the critically acclaimed YA novel *And Other Mistakes*, the editor of and a contributor to the upcoming YA horror anthology *Can't You See It's Coming?*, and a writer for the *Rainbow Fairies* early reader graphic novels. Like her two sisters, she is a proud musical-theater nerd. She lives with her family and two rescue pups, one of whom was absolutely a pandemic puppy.

Thank you for reading this Feiwel & Friends book.
The friends who made

WHEN WE ALMOST CAME UNDONE

possible are:

Jean Feiwel, Publisher
Liz Szabla, VP, Associate Publisher
Rich Deas, Senior Creative Director
Anna Roberto, Executive Editor
Holly West, Senior Editor
Kat Brzozowski, Senior Editor
Emily Settle, Senior Editor
Dawn Ryan, Executive Managing Editor
Kim Waymer, Senior Production Manager
Rachel Diebel, Editor
Foyinsi Adegbonmire, Editor
Brittany Groves, Assistant Editor
Kelly Markus, Associate Production Editor

Follow us on Facebook or visit us online at mackids.com.
Our books are friends for life.